VANITY FARE

Ann Birstein

PublishAmerica
Baltimore

© 2009 by Ann Birstein.
All rights reserved. No part of this book may be reproduced, stored in a retrieval system or transmitted in any form or by any means without the prior written permission of the publishers, except by a reviewer who may quote brief passages in a review to be printed in a newspaper, magazine or journal.

First printing

All characters in this book are fictitious, and any resemblance to real persons, living or dead, is coincidental.

PublishAmerica has allowed this work to remain exactly as the author intended, verbatim, without editorial input.

ISBN: 1-60836-391-0 (softcover)
ISBN: 978-1-4489-0248-4 (hardcover)
PUBLISHED BY PUBLISHAMERICA, LLLP
www.publishamerica.com
Baltimore

Printed in the United States of America

Books by Ann Birstein

Vanity Fare
What I Saw at the Fair
The Last of the True Believers
The Rabbi on Forty-seventh Street
American Children
Dickie's List
Summer Situations
The Sweet Birds of Gorham
The Troublemaker
Star of Glass

Acknowledgements

Many thanks:
To the Virginia Center for the Creative Arts
To Tonya Garcia, for her invaluable assistance

1

Usually, I never remember how I met somebody. In this case I did because it seemed so incredible afterward that Charlotte and I had once been strangers. But there we were, the scene forever clear in my mind: two couples on a cold winter's night in 1974, going up in an elevator, pretty sure they were on their way to the same party, but not sure what they were supposed to do about it. The husbands finally gave each other a stiff once-over, then stared at the elevator door. The wives eyed each other a bit longer, I offering a brief smile. Ordinarily, I would have gone on to introduce Peter and me on the spot. But I had no particular interest in meeting this pair. The husband, a man in his fifties, a bit portly, a bit pompous, I took to be a stockbroker. The wife, more or less the same age, was tall, thin, and draped in a gorgeous black mink coat. Her brown, subtly hennaed hair was done up in a slick French knot, which made her look very society, but a touch dated, as did the small gleaming pearls at her ears. I had seen pictures of such women at charity dinners, museum openings. Sponsors of the arts, ladies who lunched. But it didn't figure that this couple, who were not only older but clearly in another tax bracket from the rest of us, should be on their way to Herb Lobel's party, Herb being not only a psychiatrist but one with a literary bent. On the other hand, since his divorce Herb's parties had become more and more eclectic, a grab bag of old friends, who weren't particularly friends of each other, with an occasional new face thrown in. Peter and I, of course, were in the old face category since Peter and Herb had been Columbia classmates and when I came trotting across the street from Barnard the three of us often hung out together, I as a kind of sidekick.

The door to Herb's apartment was open. He was caught in the foyer between guests coming in and going out and laughed when he saw the four of us, for no particular reason, except that Herb had a habit of laughing for no particular reason.

"Have you people met?" he asked, laughing harder, a skinny little guy set on being amiable.

"We came up together in the elevator," I said. Herb nodded, then turned elsewhere, leaving us to introduce ourselves. They were Steve and Charlotte Aaronson, we were Peter and Lish Lasker. That established, we drifted into the bedroom, deposited our coats on Herb's overloaded bed, then separately made our way toward Herb's living room. It was small and low-ceilinged, typical of a high-rise East Side apartment, including Bloomingdale's furniture, and already it was clear that the party inside was crushingly and terminally dull. Unfortunately, Herb's parties always were. Guests sat pinioned to leatherette chairs and couches, or made desultory chit chat standing up, drinks in hand. No one in sight was having a good time.

"Why does Herb keep giving these parties?" I whispered to Peter. "And why do we keep going?"

"Come on, Lish," Peter said, smiling. "They're not that bad."

But they were. They never even celebrated anything, including tonight's, which was vaguely planted in the new year. I supposed they were merely meant to signal Herb's social viability as a newly single man. The second question—why did we come, why did any of us come?—Peter was no longer in a position to discuss, since he had already launched himself into the fray. But the answer to that was simple too, I supposed. We all liked Herb, and also we were as eager to reassure him that his divorce hadn't changed anything as he was to reassure himself. But it had, of course, since instead of his wife, at each party there was another very eager young, or not so young, woman in the background. I didn't think of him that way, but I guessed he was a catch.

Tonight's candidate for his hand was a slim weary-looking blonde who worked at some avant garde publishing house—or was it a little magazine? Glamorous looking, but with a little dead mouse inside. I spoke to her for a few minutes and found absolutely nothing interesting about her. Then I checked on Peter some distance away, engrossed in conversation. He looked charming, as usual, and confirmed how lucky I was not to be myself on the prowl. After that I spoke to a few people I always spoke to at Herb's, but whose names it was too late in the game to ask, and was snubbed by a few others who didn't remember who I was, including a TV producer and his snooty wife, who always looked as if they were slumming, but always came. I saw an opening on a couch. Going to sit down meant that I was throwing in the sponge, that it was next to the thin, aging socialite of the elevator encounter meant that I would be stuck there, bored, until it was time to go home. But, then, it beat trying to circulate at this dismal affair. And I did pride myself on being interested in people from all walks of life. Herb's witless girlfriends excluded.

My couch mate gave me a little nod.

"Charlotte Aaronson," she said, extending her hand.

"Lish Lasker."

It was courteous of her to have repeated her name, but then I had known at first glance that she was well-bred. This close-up confirmed it. Her dress, black, was beautifully cut, with a small diamond pin up near one shoulder. Her long tapering feet were shod in elegant black suede pumps. (Shod was not a word I normally used, but in this case it seemed called-for.) I was impressed by what all that quiet elegance must have cost. I was even more impressed by, not to say madly jealous of, the thinness of her. Her fingers were thin and tapered too, ending in the surprise of long bright red nails. The nails struck a strange note in a woman so quietly dressed, as if they had popped out of a suppressed psyche as ten red exclamation points. They were also so long they must have rendered her hands useless. But then I had pegged her from the very beginning as idle rich.

"Have you known Herb long?" I said, trying to fill up the slack.

"Long?" She shrugged. "I suppose so… My husband's a psychiatrist too." So much for the stockbroker theory. I amended it to she had bought him his practice. "And you?"

"Forever, it seems like," I said, realizing what a dumb question it had been to begin with. "My husband teaches literature at Columbia," I said. "He and Herb met there as undergraduates originally." I didn't add that they had both studied with the late great Edward Maxwell, and that Peter now administered the prestigious Edward Maxwell Prize, since she probably wouldn't know who or what that was. "He and Herb are going to give a seminar together in the spring. On sexual attitudes and the Victorians. Herb's very literary, you know."

She smiled. "Yes, I do know."

The next dumb question hung in the air, which was what did we do? She, probably nothing except the charity stuff, so I didn't ask.

"And do you teach at Columbia too?" she said politely.

Was she kidding? That bastion of male supremacy? Even if I had a PhD, which I didn't, even if there weren't nepotism rules, it wouldn't have been possible.

"I'm a writer," I said coolly.

And sat back with a falsely modest smile, waiting for the usual… "Oh? Would I ever have read anything you've written?…I've always wanted to be creative myself, but I have no time…" (Sheer lack of time seemed to be what kept most people from being writers.)… "Boy, do I have material for you…" Etc, etc. But, though interested, my couch mate didn't seem swept away.

"I write novels," I said, playing my trump. Unfortunately, it was also something of an exaggeration. I had published a number of short stories, but only one novel, an uneasy making fact, since my second novel wasn't getting off the ground. In fact, the several chapters I had sent to my agent had come back that very morning with the delicate comment that everyone felt it needed more work. Since she worked alone in her office, I didn't even know who everyone was.

"A novelist," she murmured. "Lish Lasker. Would I have—?"

"No, probably not," I said, coming clean in spite of myself. "It's Alicia Morris, actually...And my last book was probably the best suppressed publishing event since Ulysses."

"Oh, sweetie," she said, laughing, putting me off with this term of endearment. It was one thing to make fun of myself, quite another to be sympathized with by a stranger.

"And you?" I asked coldly, sending the ball back into her court.

"I'm a writer too."

"Oh? And you write—?"

"Novels," she admitted, with that rueful smile. I could imagine them piled up in her trunk. I, at least, was published, however furtively. I didn't have to ponder the name Aaronson. There was no woman novelist named Aaronson that I knew of.

"Charlotte Burns," she said, smiling even more ruefully.

Oh, my god! Charlotte Burns, author of the famous best seller of the early sixties, Vanity Fare. A novel that had made a tremendous impression on all us incipient feminists ten years ago. No wonder she had looked familiar. I must have seen her picture a million times. But with a different look, like a former debutante. Yes, I remembered her now from those photographs, terribly well bred, smiling, her teeth slightly crooked, her careful page boy held in place by two small barrettes at either side of her head, modest pearls around her neck as well as at her ears. But there had been no other books since then, though rumors surfaced from time to time that another big one was in the works, possibly a sequel.

It didn't matter. Vanity Fare was enough of a contribution for anyone to make. The definitive feminist novel, though it wasn't universally recognized as such until later. The first one to say here it is, here we are, stuck in the ghetto of our kitchens no matter what else we and the world pretend is going on, servicing our men in bed, our children out of it. Dishing up food for love. But what made it work was that it was no grim polemic. But very funny, a domestic comedy of the highest order, compared in its day with the work of Jane Austen, who had come out of the closet as a serious, major writer around the same time. Male critics hated it, sales soared. Later, I had tried to get Peter to read it, and he had sighed, then smiled indulgently, a moment that still rankled. Maybe, now that she had appeared in the flesh, I could finally get Peter interested. Because even if she had written nothing else since then, Charlotte Burns had earned her keep in the world of letters by writing Vanity Fare. And, oh, the gorgeous chuztpah of the title!

All of this translated into my blurting out, "Listen, I'm a great admirer of yours."

"Really?"

"Oh, yes." God, could I put this without sounding trite? "...Vanity Fare was the first thing I ever read that really reflected the female sensibility. I remember thinking, yes, this is how women really are." Also, screw you, Dr. Freud, though I didn't say that.

"Really?" she repeated. She shook her head modestly. It was true modesty. She clearly didn't want to hear any more hymns of praise in her honor.

"Well, who are your favorite women writers?" I asked. "Besides, obviously, Jane Austen."

"Oh, my. That's like being asked who your friends are, and suddenly you can't remember ever having any." She laughed. "I suppose, most of all, Colette."

"Most of all, Colette? You love her too?" I said, excited that we had found a common passion.

"I adore her."

"Do you remember the part about her mother and the cactus?" I asked.

"When Sido wouldn't come up to Paris to see Colette because the cactus was about to bloom?"

"For the first time in seven years, and she refused to miss it."

"That sounds so tough, doesn't it?" Charlotte said. "Modern mothers are supposed to be on tap at all times."

VANITY FARE

"But Colette was proud of her."

"She was, wasn't she?" Charlotte said, ruefully. Clearly we were talking about ourselves as mothers too, but also saying that our own mothers were nothing to boast about, the kind of subtext that brings women together. I think it was my first inkling that Charlotte Burns and I might become friends.

We were still deep in literary passions after Peter had wandered by and been introduced and Herb our host had expressed delight that we had found each other, and Steve began to make smiling let's go home signals. When the signals increased in frequency, Charlotte shrugged at me apologetically and stood up. I thought of the husband in her book, who was a smarmy climber. Her real husband, Steve, on the other hand, seemed quite agreeable. I didn't want to pursue this tack. I hated it when people came at my own fiction that way. Not that many people came at it one way or the other.

I stood up too, to go and join Peter.

"This is the first time I've ever enjoyed myself at one of Herb's parties," I said, shaking Charlotte's hand.

"I know what you mean, sweetie," Charlotte said, laughing.

Peter wasn't exactly swept away by the news of whom I'd actually been talking to, though I went on and on about it in the taxi going home. Intellectual snob at work, though he would have denied it with his dying breath. It wasn't just that Charlotte Burns had earned her literary reputation in almost exclusively female circles, but that she was a popular writer to boot. And the last popular female writer Peter had held in high esteem was Mrs. Gaskell. I didn't count in any of this, being married to him. Supporting my work was all mixed up with being husbandly. But if Peter really intended to wear the late great critic Edward Maxwell's mantle, or carry his torch, or whatever the latest platitude was that he and the widow Maxwell were exchanging, he really ought to have been more open in his tastes.

"Yes, you definitely should read Vanity Fare," I said. "If only for historic reasons."

"Okay," Peter said. "I will."

He had made such promises before, and in this case was clearly humoring me. But it was the best I could do at the moment.

We came home to an empty apartment. Our thirteen-year-old son Joey was out at the movies with some friends. There was no need for dinner since there had been deli cold cuts at Herb's. I always felt sexy after a party. This time, on account of the excitement of meeting Charlotte Burns and having her clearly like me, I was even more turned on. Peter was standing at the hall closet in his lined raincoat, plaid muffler open at the neck. I threw my arms around him. Luck was with me all the way tonight. His face was cold and delicious to the touch. Sometimes I could hardly believe this guy was my husband, he so totally corresponded to all my young daydreams when I was growing up in Queens. There was always so much sloppy emotion in my house, a constantly complaining mother, a long suffering father that what I fantasized about was civility, deference to other people's feelings. When I read Gone with the Wind, it was Ashley Wilkes I fell in love with, not Rhett Butler.

And then my sophomore year at Barnard—I was to have the best of educations, but at a girl's school, not too far from Forest Hills—I went to a party at Columbia and there was Peter, handsome, blond, the model of courtesy and grace, my very own (Jewish) Ashley. Not that I thought of myself as slender, lovely, quiet Melanie. I was short, forever on the cusp of overweight, and unable to keep my mouth shut on any subject. But Peter hadn't minded. I made him smile. He was smiling now.

We started toward the bedroom but didn't get very far. I unzipped his fly, he stuck his cold hand down my dress. We barely made it to the living room sofa. I wondered if Charlotte Burns and her husband still made love.

To my amazement she called me the next morning. Peter, much doted on, had socked Joey fraternally in the shoulder and left for his

first class, and Joey was taking a long last look into the refrigerator.
"Lish?...Charlotte Aaronson."

For a moment I was completely at sea, I had gotten so used to calling her Burns in my mind.

"Who?...Oh, what a nice surprise." I waved goodbye to Joey, who had picked up his heavy green bookbag but continued to hang around, his curiosity piqued. I wished he would leave, though there was nothing private about what Charlotte was saying. She merely wanted, she explained, to send me a copy of Vanity Fare since there was no reason on earth why I should already own one. She had me there. I was too embarrassed to say that I used to own one—it had once practically been my bible—but that I had lost it somewhere along the line. I said that I would be honored to receive a copy from her.

"Honored," she repeated, laughing. "Okay. But, Lish, in return would you send me your latest? If you have any extras."

Latest. That was a kind way of putting "only." And yes, I had a few extras, quite a few, all well on their way to being collector's items. But I was also shy about sending her one. "You don't really want to read it," I said.

"Of course, I do, sweetie," Charlotte answered, "I'm looking forward to it," and hung up.

Joey was still all ears, and looking at me skeptically. "New lover, Ma?"

"Charlotte Burns," I said distinctly. "Whom you have probably never heard of."

"Okay. Who is she?"

"A writer."

"So? You and Daddy know lots of writers. What's the big deal?"

"She's special," I said, not wanting to go into the history of the pioneers of women's liberation. Nor to add that such writers as I had met personally was as a faculty wife attending readings. Which was to say as the lowliest figure on the academic totem pole. Which was, in turn, to say that the operative word in Joey's question was "Daddy."

"Forget it," I said, taking the traditional mother's way out, which I had once sworn never to do. "Go to school."

Joey shrugged and let me kiss him goodbye, a little dubiously, a little sadly as if I had spiritually abandoned him, when, of course, at thirteen he was on the verge of abandoning me. He was dark haired like me, skinny like my late father, after whom he was named, still pint-sized and waiting around for his voice to change. I didn't like to think about the other changes in store for us both. I also didn't think Peter would be much help there. He was very palsy with Joey, but more like an older brother than a father. Sometimes I felt like the mother of both of them, but a nice mother, one that Charlotte and the women's movement would approve of.

Still musing over Charlotte's call, I made the beds, dusted in the living room, sentimentally smoothing over last night's erotic dent in the couch, and cleaned up the breakfast dishes. I picked up the newspaper from the table, where Peter had left it, briefly distracted by the latest on the eighteen minutes of missing tape. Duplicity piled on duplicity. Where would it end? And how had Nixon been elected in the first place? Not that the foreign news was much better. A ferry boat sank in Asia, an airplane exploded over Turkey. Many casualties. The usual.

More depressed than distracted, I spread out my work on the dining room table, having first taken my electric portable from the sideboard and plugged it in. I wondered if Charlotte worked directly on a typewriter too, but could more easily see her writing in longhand and then airily giving it to a secretary to transcribe. I realized also that Charlotte hadn't suggested we get together, which was strange. Maybe she would, after the exchange of books. I tried not to wonder how she would like mine. And what about this new one I was trying to plod ahead with now, totally discouraged by my agent's tepid response? I reminded myself that my other novel had once existed in the same pitiable condition, but though I believed that with my head I didn't with my heart. It was easy to forget pain, and all I could remember at this point was the thrill and power of those final revisions the last time, dotting i's, crossing t's with an unshakable certitude. Revelation had followed upon revelation. A transcendent joy right up there with sex. Here on my dining room table, however, there was no joy of any kind. Only cold empty pages waiting to be filled. I wondered if I could ask Charlotte Burns for literary advice, or would that be an imposition? I really had no one else to turn to. Peter, for husbandly reasons, was out. My agent, a depressing woman even when she didn't mean to be depressing, had small glasses and huge teeth, and began her letters to me, "Lish, dear." The magazines which accepted my work had names like Hindsight or Pioneer Quarterly. The small publishing house of George C. Crutchworth, which had done my first and only novel, was housed in an office straight out of Dickens. And who could tell if even lowly Crutchworth would ultimately want this second book? God, what wouldn't I have given to be famous, like Charlotte Burns, have a book on the all-time best seller list, be excerpted in anthologies, be famous for not granting interviews. Joey would be thrilled, though maybe Peter would have to be reassured. Or would it be the other way around? In any case, maybe by that time Charlotte Burns and I would be intimates, and she would be able to give me advice on how to handle it all.

These bright visions of the future lasted until I actually got down to work. Then characters began mumbling, refused to get into bed with one another. I couldn't imagine what they'd do when they got in there, anyhow. After all, how many apertures were there in the human body? You couldn't really count ears. Since I was already in the diningroom, what we were going to have for dinner became a more and more pressing question. Yes, my life was still Vanity Fare, with emphasis on the "fare." I was a woman in charge of two male appetites. Accomplish what I would during the day, at night they were hungry. Screwing up my courage, I packed my first novel into a padded paper bag to send to Charlotte, looking on it by now as a sad souvenir of a lost talent. ("I had it once, baby," Fitzgerald had said to anyone who would listen.) Classnotes of a Dreamer. Even if Charlotte loved it, this one novel might still only have been a fluke.

On my way to the post office, I crossed the Columbia campus. Modest little Barnard College for females, and my young womanhood were behind me on the other side of Broadway. Here, as always, I had stepped into a male fiefdom. Never mind that the place had not so long ago been busted up by activists in the peace movement—mostly guys, of course, with an assist from a compliant girl. ("Can any of you chicks type?") Today's collegians were hearty, red-cheeked, and bareheaded, with long Columbia mufflers wound around their throats. Older, professorial types, who had once posed as revolutionaries, walked along complacently trailing pipe smoke. Even the steps of Low Library suggested the path to the highest pinnacle of male achievement. Yes, the basic situation remained. Women might have been granted some small consolations in the last few years, but men still had the power. Good line. I must remember to use it somewhere. Maybe one day tell Charlotte Burns.

"Hi, Lish! How's it going?"

It was my old friend Rhoda Garfunkel, also crossing the campus, and also catching up on errands. Her arms were full of packages and shopping bags. It was not the only way our lives had run parallel over the years. We had met as Barnard freshmen, and met again in later life when both our husbands turned out to be Columbia professors. When our kids were born—her Melissa was just about the same age as my Joey—we had clocked up long hours together at the playground in Riverside Park. After that, we had drifted apart, not too far, though, since now that I was more or less a full time writer, Rhoda had become a devoted fan. (My only fan, if I wanted to be honest about it.) Every tidbit of my literary life impressed and fascinated her—a story published in one of those obscure literary journals, a meeting with my agent, a short review in the Library Journal. And, naturally, I kept dropping these tidbits into her hands, the way our kids did their apple cores in the playground. This time, I shifted the book mailer so that it couldn't help but catch her eye. "Sending your novel to someone?" she asked obligingly.

"As a matter of fact, I am." I turned it so that she could see the name and address.

"Charlotte Burns!"

"I ran into her at a party the other day," I said casually, "and she asked to see it."

"Charlotte Burns," Rhoda repeated with awe. "I thought she was dead."

"Rhoda, for god's sakes," I said. That was something I kept forgetting about my only fan. She was stupid. "Of course Charlotte Burns isn't dead. Why should she be dead?"

"Well, didn't she write Vanity Fare? Ages ago?"

"So?"

"I don't remember her writing anything else," Rhoda said, deflating a bit.

Neither did I. But that was hardly the point.

"The point is," I said, "that Vanity Fare was a groundbreaking feminist work."

The word feminist deflated Rhoda even further. (Never mind groundbreaking.) She had always been cute rather than pretty, with black curly hair and big eyes, and now she practically looked like Betty Boop. I could see her hastily counting her blessings, husband, child, etc. and not wanting to risk any of them in the service of finding herself, though sometimes she talked vaguely of going to library school.

I changed the subject. "How's Melissa?" I said.

"Oh, a typical teenager," Rhoda said happily, relaxing a bit.

"It would be great to see her one of these days," I lied. "I can't imagine where the time's flown… Well, I'd better be getting on. I'm meeting Peter for tea later with Sylvia Maxwell."

"Sylvia Maxwell?" Rhoda said, getting impressed all over again.

I wasn't up for another round. "Listen, let's get together one of these days, okay? We'll give each other a call."

"Great."

I hurried on. A few minutes later, I came out of the post office, having mailed my book first class and, partly on account of Rhoda, with a deepening sense of doubt. Then I dropped into a nearby supermarket, heavily Puerto Rican in flavor, where I picked up a pound and a half of ground chuck, and from among mounds of plantains and mangoes, three baking potatoes, and an icy lettuce. Back home again, I slapped together a meatloaf, a sure sign of hitting bottom, culinarily speaking, and scrubbed the potatoes. The lettuce I looked at thoughtfully. When we were first married, Peter used to participate in making dinner, at least making the salad. Those days were pretty much gone. They seemed to have vanished when he first started to talk about tenure, though I really couldn't put an exact date on it. I went into the dining room, cleared the table of my writing paraphernalia, and set three places for dinner. From the sideboard, my electric portable, cord dangling, and my pile of manuscript looked like exiles.

No time to brood about it though. It was now almost four, the hour, as I had told Rhoda, when I was due for tea next door at the Claremont Avenue domain of Sylvia Maxwell—domain, I always thought, because the more lowly word apartment hardly suggested the flavor of the place. It seemed to have taken shape early in Edward Maxwell's career, when he was still known chiefly as an expert in Victorian literature, and hadn't yet evolved as America's major critic of literature in general. Victorian suited Sylvia better anyhow. I think she saw herself as a kind of nineteenth century femme savante. Certainly she loved all the gewgaws of the period. Gilt-framed portraits of spurious ancestors, carved settees, cranberry glass paperweights saying such things as Brighton 1890, fluted etageres, enamel snuff boxes. "Objets trouves," Sylvia Maxwell airily and mistakenly called this junk.

She herself, when I came in, was presiding over a butler's table laden with a formal silver tea service, and gazing benevolently at

VANITY FARE

Peter, who was eating a raisin scone. I took my place guiltily, like a late student, beside Peter on the settee. Actually, I didn't know why my presence was required, since it really wasn't a social occasion. They were only going to talk, as usual, about Edward Maxwell's literary effects, and specifically the Maxwell Prize, which Peter administered—a feather in the cap of an academic so young. Not that Peter would have said a word of reproach if I hadn't shown up. It was like making dinner. Expected, but not a matter of being actually coerced. Of course, in the old days Sylvia Maxwell had been a holy terror, especially to a young faculty wife. A terror, actually, to all other women, whom she held in scorn. The grande dame of all time. Now she was half-blind and almost powerless. An old rooster in a shiny black dress. But still scary, damn it. As always I had to remind myself that Sylvia Maxwell's celebrity, such as it was, derived solely from the fame of her husband. That she had done absolutely nothing on her own, except write terrible little literary essays which got published solely through Edward's connections, and outraged letters to the Times about some political event or other. Yet she had successfully browbeaten the literary world at large into thinking she was someone too. Maybe in fact that was the source of her ferocious and insistent egotism, the inner tickle that kept reminding her that without her husband she was nothing.

"Peter, darling," Sylvia said, having taken her eyes off him just long enough to quickly hand me a cup of tea—lemon, no sugar. "You are such a comfort to me in this dark hour."

"I'm happy to hear that," Peter said.

What dark hour? Edward had already been dead for five years, and his widow was safely and permanently ensconced in a large low rent Columbia apartment, with all kinds of people trooping in day and night to render her homage. Just for the hell of it, I tried to imagine Sylvia sucking Edward off in their heyday, and failed. Then I tried to imagine her having an affair with one of his colleagues and failed there too. No, there was no use trying to normalize her. From there, my mind inevitably went on to Peter. Had he had affairs since we'd been married? I would probably never know, since Ashley Wilkes would hardly kiss and tell. Maybe with a graduate student or two, they were so easy and willing, like fish in a barrel. Peter wouldn't have taken more trouble than that. As for me, yes, I had been seriously tempted as a married woman, early on and for a short time, when the juices ran high and I spent most of my time diapering Joey. But this hadn't happened in years. It wasn't a solution. To be more precise, it hadn't defined the problem.

"And what are you up to these days, my dear?" Sylvia Maxwell asked, unexpectedly recalling my existence.

"What?"

Quickly collecting myself, I thought of saying that I had gone back to drinking tea in a glass, as had my grandfather and his fathers before him. Instead, I said, enunciating clearly as if to a deaf person and as if it were news, "I am writing a novel."

Sylvia sighed and nodded sadly, as if this were a harbinger of the death of civilization. Peter gave only a quick guilty glance in my direction.

"And now," Sylvia said, abandoning me as a subject and turning back to my husband. "Tell me what you've found that's worthy of the Maxwell Prize."

"I'm afraid nothing yet, Sylvia—"

"I'm not surprised."

"—but it's still early on," Peter continued good naturedly, though aside from the honor of it, administering the prize in addition to his own scholarly writing and teaching placed a big extra burden on him.

"Well, we can always not award a prize this year," Sylvia said. "Since, frankly, I doubt that anything deserving has been written in the last twenty years, much less twelve months." She laughed. "But then, that's why you're administering the prize, Peter, darling, not I."

"Have you ever read Vanity Fare?" I blurted out.

"Of course, I have," Sylvia said, regarding me from amidst her

VANITY FARE

Victorian paraphernalia as if I were mad.

I started to explain, but stopped. What would be the point? I would have to explain that I wasn't talking about Thackeray and then spell the title of Charlotte Burns's book, and Sylvia would be right back in her death of civilization mode.

Finally tea time was over. Peter helped Sylvia to rise and, leaning on his arm, she saw us to the door. Outside, it came as shock that we were only on Claremont Avenue, not in Bloomsbury.

"The woman's ludicrous," I said, as we ducked into our own apartment building next door.

"Oh, come on, Lish. Whatever you once thought of her, she's only a harmless old lady now."

Were we talking about the same person? Still, I admired Peter for sticking to his guns. I always liked seeing Peter in his Ashley, courtly mode. In truth the handsome son of an ugly mother, and therefore a permanent sucker for an aging woman with a sob story. Would I have preferred him to kick elderly widows of colleagues downstairs? Hell, he was even sweet to my mother when she came up from Florida, which was more than I could be. Still basking in tender feelings toward him, I opened a bottle of red wine and poured us each a glass to have while dinner finished cooking. It would take a while, but then we had just come from tea. Peter took his wine into his study along with a sheaf of student papers. From Joey's room came the sound of earsplitting rock, meaning he was home too.

Finally, I called them both to the table. Joey made a face at the meatloaf, but I stared him down until he stabbed a potato. I made another trip to the kitchen, to bring the salad, which I had forgotten, and sat down again. The meatloaf was rare in the middle, too well done around the edges. There were hard parts to the potatoes. The salad, over which I had hurriedly sloshed dressing, was drowning. So was I, in the silence. The two of them just sat there, eating away. For dessert, I brought in the rest of yesterday's store bought apple pie. Peter said he didn't want coffee. I stuck the cork in the wine bottle, got up to clear, put the dishes into the dishwasher, took out the garbage, and there they were at the diningroom table, two guys laughing about something.

"Perhaps you think I'm the live-in maid?" I said pleasantly.

They looked up, injured and ingenuous, but not surprised. Why weren't they surprised? This enraged me even more.

"Can't you even take out the garbage? What am I, gender disposed for garbage removal?"

"You should have asked me," Joey mumbled.

"This isn't a voluntary operation!"

"Take it easy, Lish," Peter said, smiling.

"According to you I'm always supposed to take it easy. The whole world is supposed to take it easy!"

I ran into the bedroom and slammed the door. Great, I told myself. Nice going, Lish. I, who only that morning had conned myself into believing I was an incipient Charlotte Burns, maybe even Colette—what the hell, maybe even another Jane Austen—had just done a grand imitation of my mother, the yenta. No, there had to be a better way.

2

Books had been exchanged and to my amazed relief Charlotte seemed sincerely impressed with mine. She called only a week after I had sent it, at the same hour as the last time, right after breakfast, when Peter had just gone off to his campus office, and Joey was on his way to school—as if she knew when I would be free to talk.

"It's very fine, Lish. Very literary. A true coming of age novel."

"Really?" Actually, Classnotes of a Dreamer was about two college lovers who were already of age. But why quarrel with such a flattering appraisal?

"You're very wise to avoid big flashy effects."

"I am?"

"I can see where you'd be a superb short story writer—how wonderfully you deal with the glancing moment. I look forward to reading the collection of your stories too."

"Well, they haven't been collected yet."

"I'm sure they will be. I really envy you that gift, Lish. I'm a lousy short story writer myself."

"Come on, Charlotte. Anyhow, you're a fabulous novelist. Nobody can be everything. I mean Vanity Fare was certainly—"

"How's the teaching?" Charlotte interrupted.

"I don't teach," I said, startled by the abrupt change of subject until I remembered how truly modest she was whenever Vanity Fare came up.

"I meant your husband's," Charlotte said, with some embarrassment.

"This is intersession."

"Right. Sorry, I forgot. I've lost touch with higher education..." She was clearly searching for something to say. Finally she came up with, "Herb Lobel tells me that your husband is Edward Maxwell's literary executor."

"No, that's Maxwell's widow. Peter is the administrator of the Maxwell Prize."

"But you must have known him well."

"Edward Maxwell? Well, of course, Peter knew him better. I liked him, though. He was very courtly, very charming. Handsome too, in fact. The relict, alas, is another matter."

"Oh?"

I told Charlotte a bit about Sylvia's grande dame airs and the fake Victoriana, and the terrible tea parties, not that I thought Charlotte would really care, though she was kind enough to laugh.

"Naturally, when I tried to mention your book to the great lady she thought I was talking about Thackeray."

Charlotte gave another small laugh and, clearly uninterested, changed the subject again.

"Listen, Lish, this will probably bore the hell out of you, but I'm having a few people in for drinks in a couple of weeks. Nothing of any great consequence, but maybe you and your husband would like to come. I'll send you an invitation. Okay?"

More than okay. I felt I had won some contest I hadn't even entered. Even when the invitation itself came a few days later it didn't dim my enthusiasm, though the return address said C. Aaronson, which was dismaying as well as surprising, and the card had little bubbly cocktail glasses on it. Maybe this was her doctor-husband's taste, or maybe her social secretary's. Who knew what the domestic order was in the home of a best selling novelist?

"On the other hand," I said to Peter, "it does have a certain comfortably traditional feel to it. Like rice pudding, almost. Maybe that's what she was after. Inverse sophistication."

"Why are you so impressed with her?" Peter said. "You've met well known writers before."

VANITY FARE

Same question as Joey's, both of them sidestepping the fact that it was as wifey ignored at the official dinner beforehand, smiling brightly when finally introduced. Ignored once more.
"This is different. This is personal. Charlotte Burns had a great impact on my life long before she and I met." This one's mine, I wanted to shout, mine!
Peter looked exceedingly dubious. I stared him down. "Okay, I'll read her book," Peter said.

Actually, it was a party, a big party, not a few people in for drinks, and an important occasion too. It had something to do with Vanity Fare being made into a movie, which was news to me. Charlotte had never mentioned it, and if it had been in the papers that was before I met Charlotte, and therefore hadn't made any impression on me.
"But this is great," I said to Charlotte. "You must be so excited."
"Sweetie," she said, with her familiar moue, "it's all so long after the original event."
"That just proves you were way ahead of your time," I said. But she had already drifted off into her sea of guests.
I looked around, openly impressed. What an apartment. An enormous living room, with pale furniture, ivory silk drapes, an occasional paisley throw, a few elegant and slender gilded antique tables. Beautiful, tasteful, not quite lived in. A terrace with a stunning, twinkling night view of the city at the far end. A suggestion of infinite numbers of rooms beyond this one. The guest bathroom, where I had immediately gone to repair myself, had coordinated gold-striped wall paper and towels. This maybe impressed me most. Nobody in our academic circles had a guest bathroom, much less a coordinated one. The whole place was carefully planned and executed, no doubt by an army of decorators.
And then there was the guest list. Dozens of distinguished literary figures I had only heard of or seen pictures of, but never laid eyes on. Kurt Vonnegut, shabbier and slouchier but also kindlier looking than

I expected, Sam Cuccio, the ultimate macho novelist, radiating an impenetrable aura of permanent tan and celebrity, Sunny Mansfield, another novelist of Charlotte Burns's generation, along with her husband, the (self-proclaimed) "great poet" David Harvey, who seemed to be laying down the law to some cowed woman, a dapper man in a white suit who I thought might be Gay Talese, Mort Glasgow, a famous book editor, Saint Swithin, angry playwright of the sixties, Nancy Tarkov, a journalist whose picture I recognized from the contributors list of Ms, Karl Brach, the director of Vanity Fare, whose last film—not movie—about a lonely New England spinster and her clandestine affair with an American Indian lover had made him much talked about. Obviously the plight of the desperate woman was an idea that intrigued him.

Anyway, they were all exceedingly well known and not exactly in their first youth, including Karl Brach, a plump man who had stuffed himself into tight jeans and a leather jacket. Otherwise, the only generational exceptions were an occasional tall gorgeous wife, Herb Lobel, who was now reaching new heights of amiability as as he circulated among the guests, and of course Peter and me. To my amazement, the notorious Sam Cuccio showed signs of advancing in my direction. I was wondering what I could possibly say to him when Charlotte's husband Steve materialized at my side to ask how I was getting along, and Sam Cuccio smiled and veered off.

"Not too bored, I hope," Steve Aaronson said. He was tall and pleasantly owlish, with rimless eyeglasses. A typical looking Jewish doctor.

"Bored? God, no," I said. "I'm impressed out of my mind."

"With what?"

"The guest list, for one thing."

"Ah, my swan," Steve said, shaking his head affectionately. At that point a young woman whom I hadn't noticed before, sweet and scared looking, wandered over to him.

"Cindy!" Steve said, his face lighting up, and introduced me to his and Charlotte's daughter. In a faint whispery voice, she said hello to me, and vanished. I had almost forgotten Charlotte had a daughter—in our conversations she had alluded to her only a few times, in passing—and now, seeing Charlotte with Peter, I made my way to them to tell Charlotte how lovely Cindy was.

"Cynthia," Charlotte corrected me. "Yes, she is lovely, isn't she?" she agreed, though without wild enthusiasm.

Charlotte looked nothing like the way she had at Herb's that first night, or how I imagined her when we talked over the phone. In fact, she was almost the epitome of the popular notion of a best-selling lady novelist, in an emerald green dress with a short pouffed skirt, skinny shoulders bare except for thin spaghetti straps, head thrown back, elegant French knot intact. It was not an altogether flattering get up. In fact, it made her look a bit drawn, a little over the hill, like the rest of her guests. But for that reason more vulnerable, somehow more likeable.

Brushing the matter of Cynthia politely aside—who must have been well into her twenties, I realized, in spite of the girlish air—Charlotte asked Peter about his Columbia courses. "I understand that you and Herb were Columbia undergraduates together," she said.

"Yes, but Herb got an A, I got a B," Peter said, laughing.

"That's hard to believe," Charlotte said, laughing too, "considering that you're now Edward Maxwell's literary executor, Lish tells me."

"Only the administrator of the Maxwell Prize," Peter corrected her. Unfazed, she went on to talk about how much Maxwell's work, particularly The Ambiguous Arrow, had meant to her. Which was surprising until I realized that Edward had first risen to prominence during Charlotte's college years at Gorham—or had she said Vassar? (And had she also hinted at graduating summa, or was that only my imagination?) No matter. Charlotte was obviously just being polite. It was, after all, an incongruous conversation to be having amid all the sophisticated and glittery chatter in her very posh apartment. Yes, indeed, we were very far off from the dreary groves of academe.

"Nancy Tarkov," a woman's voice said to me.

I turned around. "Oh. How do you do. I'm very pleased to meet you...I'm Lish Lasker...Alicia Morris."

"I know," Nancy Tarkov said, smiling. I was flattered. Obviously Charlotte had mentioned me to her. I knew she was Charlotte's friend, though she had none of Charlotte's panache, but was quite coarse-looking in fact, with kinky black hair, a short wide nose, and a gap between her front teeth. Her smile was meant to be friendly, but it made me nervous.

"Charlotte says your book's great," she told me.

"Well, Charlotte's very kind."

"Women never learn, do they?" Nancy Tarkov said, shaking her head.

"Learn what?"

"Not to be falsely humble."

Clearly that wasn't anything this woman was suffering from.

"I'm sincerely humble," I said. "There's a difference."

She didn't laugh. "You ought to join our group."

"What group? You mean a consciousness-raising group? Thanks, but I don't think so."

I had gone through so much of that already, I wasn't up for a sequel. Not that I'd retreated from my feminist position. I'd marched for abortion rights, I'd march again for ERA. But those first small groups, thrilling at first, had been too intimate, too searing, had opened too many still raw wounds.

"We don't talk about personal problems," Nancy Tarkov said, understanding my reluctance. "We address purely professional matters."

"Oh? Is Charlotte a member?"

"Charlotte's not a joiner," Nancy said, with that smile that suggested she was in possession of some privileged information.

Then that settled it. I wasn't a joiner, either. After all, Charlotte was one of the most committed feminists of us all. Not only in her

VANITY FARE

work, but in areas where it mattered. I mean, take even the simple fact of my being here. I was delighted that Charlotte had been courteous to Peter. But it was only thanks to me that we had been invited to this glittering party in the first place. A fabulous first, since our social life usually emanated from Peter and faculty connections (except for Herb and he was now faculty too.) I tried to remember when this had actually had come about, and if it was at the same time Peter had stopped making the salad, but couldn't track it down. Charlotte was now shaking Peter's hand to say goodbye, and then she went off to other departing guests. The party was clearly almost over. I wondered if like other celebrities, Sam Cuccio had gone home too. But no, he was still there, the kind of personage who automatically stood out in a crowd. Perhaps he would approach again. If so, I had better think of what to say.

3

By now Charlotte and I had begun to talk on the phone at least three or four mornings a week. To my surprise Charlotte had started it—I would never have had the nerve—seeming to know by instinct, now that intersession was over, just when Peter and then Joey left and the coast was clear for a long private chat. If Peter happened to be at home, I said I'd call back, though Charlotte soon knew his teaching schedule as well as I did. After a while, I overcame my own shyness about telephoning her first thing in the morning, and was calling her almost as often as she called me. It was really just a way of touching base before the day started. She had somehow become a girlfriend in a way Rhoda never was, never could be. What we actually talked about, of course, would have been hard to say if anyone asked me, though we roamed all over the place. How unreadable Thomas Pynchon was, Patricia Hearst's kidnapping, Nixon's possible impeachment, the astonishing obtuseness of men in general.

"Really? Steve too? I thought maybe that since he's a psychiatrist…"

"Are you kidding, sweetie?…"

Actually, I knew better. I was just testing the waters. Then there was the problem of running a household and trying to be a writer at the same time, which wasn't so much arduous, we admitted, as a matter of switching hats, energy consuming and always leading to a confusion of priorities.

"And I was so sure that for young women of your generation," Charlotte said, "it would be different."

This time I asked her if she was kidding. Though frankly I was amazed that with her kind of money she didn't put the whole houskeeping situation into the hands of a ruthlessly efficient cook and butler. Or maybe she did, and maybe it was still a big pain in the ass. Naturally, we talked about sex too. But lightly—no locker room stuff. Women didn't talk that way anyhow, in my experience, though I was sure men thought we did. I also confessed to my dread of getting pregnant again, precautions and all.

"Precautions," Charlotte said amusedly. "Yours, of course. Men still aren't taking responsibility."

"I guess not."

"Oh, well, they're all fundamentally bastards, anyway."

"Not all of them," I said.

"I know, I know." She laughed. "Your husband's supportive." I wasn't happy with that adjective, it made Peter sound like a truss, but I let it go.

"How's the teaching going?" Charlotte asked, unexpectedly changing the subject, as she often did.

"You mean Peter's, I assume."

"That's right. You don't have a PhD. But Peter does?"

"Of course, he does," I said. Her obtuseness about the workings of the academy, as always, astonished me. But then, none of it really interested her. Charlotte inhabited the glitzy world of New York Magazine, and I might as well have been was talking about some kind of ant colony.

"And then he's also the executor of the Maxwell estate. He seems so young for such a heavy responsibility."

"Peter's the administrator of the Maxwell Prize," I corrected her for the nth time. "And Peter's not that young. He's almost forty."

"Oh, my," Charlotte said, "is almost forty not young?" She sounded very sad.

"Listen, who the hell knows what's young anymore?" I said quickly. "In many ways, you're one of the youngest people I know."

"Oh, sweetie, come on."

"I mean it. You're full of beans, full of conviction. Also a real spirit of generosity toward other women. Which to me is real feminism, not how many organizations you belong to. Also, you've had to battle male chauvinism at its height. I mean, take someone like Sam Cuccio..."

"Sam?" Charlotte said, laughing. "What made you think of Sam?"

"He was at your party."

"Oh? Did he come on to you?"

"Not really. He just asked me what my name was when he was leaving." I'd hysterically told him both. He'd also said it was great to see a fresh face, but it seemed impolitic to mention that at the moment.

There was a pause. Then Charlotte laughed again. Then, "Well, as you know, sweetie. It wasn't just Sam. Sam's actually harmlesss. It was the whole intellectual climate. The idea that some subjects were 'women's' subjects, and therefore simply infra dig, artistically worthless. Like motherhood, for example—"

"—and domesticity. You were the first to zero in on that one."

"Yes, well…Whereas war, violence, brutal sex—oh, yes, those were worthy subjects. And then the entire literary business was based on seduction. Male editors, male agents took you to lunch and you didn't know whether they wanted to publish you or lay you. I suppose that's still true—?"

If this was a question, unfortunately I hadn't had much experience with either.

"—God, I remember early on, a smarmy editor of some quarterly, who rejected one of my stories saying, 'Is this what you think adultery is?' As if only men had the lowdown on such subjects. Can you believe that?…And so many gifted women were the casualties of that kind of thinking…Look at poor Sunny Mansfield. Her husband beats her, you know."

"Really? And she stays with him?"

"Maybe he's stopped." She laughed. "David Harvey's getting older too."

"Well, I can't imagine you taking that kind of crap from anyone."

There was an awkward silence. Had I stumbled into something? "Or someone like Nancy Tarkov," I hastened to add. "I think you mentioned she was once married?"

"To a psychiatrist," Charlotte said ruefully. This had been the trend among Charlotte's generation of women writers. Maybe psychiatrists were the only guys willing to take them on. "But she left him. She fell in love."

"Really? Who was the lucky fellow?"

"Arlene Mott."

Arlene Mott? Oh, well, the rush to lesbianism had been another trend. "Who's Arlene Mott?"

"Editor-in-chief at Colophon Press. But she and Nancy broke up long ago...Oh, sweetie, why am I telling you all this? It's all water under the bridge anyway... I'm just having trouble with a book I've gone back to, that's all. That's why I'm rambling this way."

Trouble with a book she had gone back to? It was the first time she had mentioned it. Could this be the long-rumored big one after Vanity Fare? I was hesitant to ask.

"I can't believe that you're having trouble with any book," I said.

"Believe it."

"Isn't your editor any help?"

"My editor?"

"Mort Glasgow?"

"Oh. No, not really."

"Well, listen," I said, "for what it's worth even Edward Maxwell used to complain about off days from time to time."

"Really?" Charlotte had perked up. "How fascinating. He actually complained to you?"

"Well, actually to Peter."

We both sighed. There was that male turf thing again.

"Look, Charlotte," I said, amazed by my own sudden boldness, but the subject meant a lot to me. "I'd be glad to look over your manuscript—if you think it might help. I'm not a bad critic myself, actually."

"Why, sweetie, how kind," Charlotte said. "We'll talk." And hung up soon after.

Maybe I had overreached myself, but Charlotte hadn't sounded angry, just busy. True, we hadn't made a date to see each other, but we never did. It was the one thing I found puzzling about this new friendship—it continued to be conducted by phone. In fact, since her party over six weeks ago, Charlotte and I hadn't seen each other again. Of course, it was New York and we didn't live in the same neighborhood. Then too, as we agreed, to meet for lunch under the circumstances would only break up the day. Coffee or a drink in the afternoon ran straight into dinner time. Dinner out would involve the husbands. "And, really, Lish, who needs them?" "Nobody," I said. "Nobody." Not true, certainly in my case, but I felt guilty about contradicting her. It would be like betraying the basis of our friendship. Still, it made me wonder again whether she and her husband still made love.

Several mornings later, I had just finished agreeing with Charlotte for the umpteenth time that men could be incredibly insensitive, when the telephone rang again. I assumed it was for Peter and was all ready with my Mrs. Lasker spiel about how Professor Lasker could be reached at his campus office, and took a few more sips of coffee before I answered.

"Alicia Morris?"

My antennae shot up. It couldn't be.

"Yes? This is she." I!

"Sam Cuccio." Oh, God, it was.

My heart was pounding. I wished I weren't standing by the kitchen sink, surrounded by breakfast detritus, wearing an old Barnard sweatshirt, stray hair stuck out of the way with combs. If television telephones ever happened, I would never answer.

"You're up early," I said stupidly.

"Did you think I spent my nights carousing?" Sam asked, laughing.

"Yes."

"I have a bad press. Look, I'd like to see you."

"See me...? Oh, I don't think that's a good idea."

"Why not?"

"Well, I mean..." My mind grappled with various good reasons, all of which vanished immediately. "Isn't it obvious?"

"Not to me, dear. Spell it out."

"Well, I mean..." Where was all my hard won sophistication? Where was all my hard won anything? "We're both married!"

"And married people in the same profession can't meet and talk?" For a moment I didn't follow him. When I did it was like a small light at the end of a tunnel. "Ah, you mean that we're both writers?"

"I was under that impression."

"Well, that's true, but still—"

"Dear lady, I don't know what you imagine I have in mind. I just wanted to invite you to tea. At the Plaza, unless you hate the Plaza."

"On the contrary," I said. "I adore the Plaza. It's practically all that's left of a New York worth living in."

"Exactly my feelings. What day is good for you?"

How had this come about? But, really, where was the harm in it? What could be safer than tea amid potted palms and a string ensemble? No, Sam Cuccio was absolutely right. Of course colleagues of different sexes should be able to get together freely. I picked the following Thursday, for no reason except that it was far enough off for me to change my mind, and because Thursday had a safe ring to it too. Charlotte! Where was Charlotte? No, she would only laugh at my silly anxiety. I decided there was no point in saying anything ahead of time to Peter, either.

They were actually playing "Tea for Two." A small string ensemble sawing away, no, "rendering a selection" on a podium festooned with potted palms. It was true what I had said to Sam. I always thought of the Plaza as the last beautiful souvenir of old New

York, the Gilded Age, Henry James, Edith Wharton, with an elegant soupcon of Paris thrown in. In short, the exact opposite of my girlhood in Queens. It was to lunch at the Plaza that I had made Peter bring me on my first birthday after we were married. It was at the Plaza that Ramona and I celebrated her becoming my agent instead of my employer. It was to the Plaza years later that I took a little Joey and a littler Melissa, before a matinee of Hello Dolly. She wore tiny patent leather shoes and a pink organdy dress, Joey a miniature Eton jacket and tie. Unfortunately, in a couple of minutes the two of them were swapping vomiting in public places stories.

Actually, I was feeling pretty nauseated myself at the moment. I scanned the Palm Court anxiously. Was Sam there already, waiting at a table? If so I couldn't see him. If he were late, how long should I wait? Naturally, I had once more agonized over what to wear and settled on a slenderizing navy blue suit and a print blouse, realizing only now that I was more suitably dressed for a job interview than a tryst. But really what were the rules for this sort of thing? Maybe the height of worldliness would be to take a table and have tea by myself, even if he didn't show up. The maitre d' was looking at me with lifted eyebrow from his station at a lavish display of pastries. I felt a hand at my elbow, and turned around. Then, like Mrs. Dalloway, there Sam was.

"Waiting long?"

"No, I just got here."

"Good."

At his touch on my elbow a thrill went through me, but Sam, whose hand it was, appeared perfectly calm and casual. He didn't smell of booze either, as he was famous for doing and had at Charlotte's party. No hanky panky. It really was teatime. I was torn between relief and disappointment. The maitre d', now deferential, led us to a reserved table, not secluded but right in the middle of the room. Yes, Sam's intentions were clearly honorable, unless like a purloined letter he was hiding us out in the open. The string ensemble had stopped rendering.

VANITY FARE

I glanced around. The crowd was more tourist than fin de siecle. Several people were looking at Sam. Did they recognize him? I saw a couple of touristy nudges.

Sam was asking me what I wanted. Fortunately the occasion had taken away my appetite, so I settled for tiny tea sandwiches. Sam asked to look at the pastry cart, selected a Napoleon, pushed it away, then settled back and smiled. If he was aware of being stared at he gave no sign of it. He seemed to have eyes only for me.

"How did you get my phone number?" I asked. "From Charlotte?"

Not a brilliant opening. I didn't like his laugh. Which one of us was he laughing at? Charlotte? Me?

"I have my sources. Now, tell me about yourself."

"There's nothing to say..." He lifted an eyebrow. "No, really. I wouldn't even know where to start."

"Start somewhere, darling."

"Okay," I said. "Call me Ishmael."

Swell. Marvelous. Congratulations, Lish. I wouldn't have been surprised if Sam had got up and left right then and there. But no, he seemed to be seriously pondering my remark.

"That's interesting, what you just said. I wouldn't have thought of Moby Dick as one of your main literary influences."

"It isn't," I said. "I hate it. I think it's purely a boy's book. Though Rhoda Garfunkel née Katz and I used to have major arguments about that—whether there is or isn't a feminine sensibility?" Actually, I was the one who had been doing the arguing. Rhoda, as always, was nonplused. "Of course that was years ago."

"Rhoda Garfunkel nee Katz?"

"A college friend. We were both English majors."

"I like that," he said. "I like your not forgetting your old friends."

"I can't forget her, she lives near me—"

"And I particularly like your loyalty to Charlotte Burns."

"Loyalty? Why do you put it that way? I admire Charlotte, I admire her work."

"That's very sweet." He smiled and shrugged. "Yes, loyalty is an admirable quality in a woman."

"And in a man?"

"You don't run across it that often."

All this was the supertext. The subtext was that having eaten all the itty bitty sandwiches in sight, and further contemplated Sam's untouched Napoleon, I could no longer distract myself from the simple, overwhelming fact of his presence. The guy absolutely had charisma. That easy glorious smile, the movie star cleft in his chin, the ability to wear a dark turtle neck sweater without looking like a turtle. All this, plus the most overwhelming fact of all, that while a great deal of attention remained focused on him, I remained the sole focus of his attention. Teatime or not, there was danger here and I knew it, though Sam certainly didn't acknowledge any, and had already lowered my defenses to the point where I had admitted to becoming a writer originally during a post partum depression. Hardly seduction material. Nevertheless, here I was in an intimate tete a tete with Sam Cuccio, world famous novelist and womanizer, who had singled me out for reasons unknown. It didn't help that the string ensemble was now playing "Stranger in Paradise."

I pulled myself together and asked him about him, though I really wasn't interested. I was too fixated on his person to care about his history. Still, it was surprising that instead of a boyhood in Little Italy, Mafia connections and all the rest of it, he came from a solid bourgeois background, the son of a doctor, raised in Providence, educated at Harvard. After graduation, he had served in Korea, and then decided to become a writer. There was a casual reference to earlier marriages—four? five?—and warmer references to the children spawned with succeeding wives. Many children. It seemed like a hobby of his, though he didn't seem the least bit paternal. Nevertheless, the multiple marriages and multiple children left me at a distinct disadvantage, since I had barely managed to eke out one of each. I really didn't like the drift of this conversation.

"You're looking around. I'm boring you," Sam said.

"What? Oh, no, not at all," I said quickly, covering my tracks. "I'm just a sucker for turn of the century grandeur. Did you know that Frank Lloyd Wright stayed in this very hotel whipping delightedly through the corridors in his cape the whole time he was despoiling upper Fifth Avenue with that awful Guggenheim?"

"Awful Guggenheim," Sam repeated.

"It's a bunker."

"Then I take it that you don't approve of Frank Lloyd Wright?"

"No."

"And that you don't approve of me, either?"

"No."

Sam laughed, as if I had just said something utterly delightful.

"Look, it's not up to me to approve or disapprove."

"Isn't it?" He thought that over for a moment, tilting his head again, and examining my face. "Oh, Alicia—"

"Yes?"

"I'd better not keep you any longer."

"Keep me? No, really, I—"

But he had already signaled for the check, and was reaching inside his wallet. This was it? It was all over?

He propelled me through the lobby and we stood outside on the steps. Hansom cabs were drawn up along the entrance to the park. There was a sweet, heady smell of false spring and horse manure in the air.

"Can I drop you somewhere?" Sam asked. "I'm heading uptown."

"No," I said. "I'm going the other way. Anyway, I want to walk. I love to walk." I desperately needed to think this all over.

He nodded, as if in my desire to walk I combined the best attributes of all women. A taxi drew up and Sam got in.

"Thanks for the lovely tea," I said.

"Thanks for coming." He gave me a little wave through the window. I stood there, my mind working busily and fruitlessly like the idiot's in The Sound and the Fury, who kept trying to say what he couldn't.

"It was lovely," I called, as Sam sped away, "lovely!"

Though what I was trying to say was, are you disappointed? Will I see you again?

I looked at my watch. The whole thing had taken exactly an hour. I didn't know whether to laugh or cry. It was like being out on the street after a rare publishing lunch with George C. Crutchworth, hopes raised, all dressed up and nowhere to go, while everyone else went back to business. I crossed the street to Bergdorf's, wishing to linger in the shadow of the Plaza a little longer. Not that Bergdorf's was my kind of store. It would take Charlotte Burns to shop here with impunity. No, usually, I just looked at the windows while Peter and I stood on line for a movie at the Paris. Maybe now would be a good time for a movie, come to think of it—the solution to all problems. Except there wasn't a problem, only a mystery. Which was, what did Sam Cuccio want of me, or, to back up a bit, what the hell had he seen in me in the first place? True, I was about twenty years younger than he, but hardly a chick. And his latest wife, judging from my brief glimpse of her at Charlotte's party, was probably younger than I, gorgeous too. I wondered if he would ever call me again. He had made me feel simultaneously that he would and that he wouldn't. Of course, I could always call him, apologize perhaps for offending him. There was no reason why we couldn't be friends, which was what Sam had seemed to be saying he wanted. And after all, what male friends did I have, aside from Herb Lobel maybe, and he was everybody's friend? It was getting to be more and more a case for a movie, except that it would make me late for dinner, and anyway, when I looked at the Paris marquee, it was The Sting.

I did a sharp turn and marched into Bergdorf's. An hour later—as long as it had taken to have tea—I was the owner of a new, wildly overpriced black dress with thin spaghetti straps, a dress that would have made Moll Flanders sit up and take notice. I could wear it everywhere, the saleslady had assured me. Where? Where the hell could I wear it? To tea at Sylvia Maxwell's? And what had impelled me to that improbable exposure of bosom? Was I mad? I thought of slapping a fichu across my poitrine and marching into the Columbia English department office to demand an honorary Phd, and equal rights for sexy women. Yes, I was mad. How else explain why I was suddenly so deliriously happy? So in love with a spring that hadn't even come yet?

Back home, I stuck my Bergdorf's shopping bag into my jammed closet, where it burned like a guilty secret. Not that Peter cared where I shopped, or questioned what I spent, though the price of that dress would certainly make him wonder. The real guilt lay elsewhere. I took a look at myself in the mirror above my bureau to see if any of it showed. Thought of that old novelist's trick of defining character by a look in the mirror. But nothing showed at all. What I saw was a short, round faced woman with dark hair of indeterminate length which badly needed cutting or growing in or styling or something, a woman looking wary. A woman, in short, on her way to the kitchen to see about dinner.

I had called Joey from Bergdorf's and told him to heat up three frozen turkey pot pies. When I checked in the oven I found four. In the diningroom, four places were set at the table. This mystery was explained when Joey emerged from his room with Melissa, Rhoda Garfunkel's daughter, of all people, trailing behind him.

"Well, this is a surprise," I said.

"I invited her," Joey said, his voice suddenly cracking on the her.

I knew they went to the same school, and of course had known each other since childhood, but when had they become friends independent of Rhoda and me? I took another look at Melissa, and understood why from Joey's point of view they should be. Melissa was absolutely adorable, her little fanny tightly encased in bell bottom jeans, her small breasts jaunty under her big blue denim work shirt, one eye obscured by a cascade of long black curly hair. The other eye, big and blue, was opened wide.

"I hope you don't mind my being here," Melissa said, in a hushed baby voice.

"Of course not," I said untruthfully. Actually, I didn't want to cope with anything at the moment, much less burgeoning teenage sexuality. "I was asking your mother about you only the other day. Other week." Month?

"Really? Well, she talks about you all the time."

"Really?"

"Oh, yes. She remembers when you were first starting to write."

"We go back a long time." I seemed to be saying that a lot lately. "Excuse me."

I started toward the kitchen, but Joey was already emerging with the four turkey pot pies on a tray. Dear God. We sat down at the diningroom table, one big happy family—like teenage sex, the furthest thing from my mind and mood at the moment. Nevertheless it was on the tip of my tongue to apologize to Melissa for the menu, and explain that it was usually a gourmet three-course meal cooked by me from scratch. A lie, but I stupidly wanted Rhoda to get a good report.

I looked around, in case there were any complaints on this end, but Peter was smiling with idiotic delight at Melissa, an expression I had never seen on his face in connection with Joey. Had he secretly yearned for a daughter all these years? Could he be secretly hoping I'd try again? If so, he was absolutely out of luck. No, as I'd told a complaining Joey early on, it was either being an only child or an orphan. Another pregnancy and I'd shoot myself. But the product of my actual pregnancy, Joey, was wearing an idiotic smile identical to his father's. In fact he and Peter were beaming upon Melissa like a pair of chorus boys in a Ginger Rogers movie. I wished I couldn't see Sam Cuccio laughing his head off at this scene.

"Sorry about this dinner," I finally blurted out to Melissa. "Usually,

I try for something a bit more original."

"Oh, well, you're creative in other ways."

"Thank you."

"It must be wonderful to be a famous and successful writer."

Famous? Successful? Was she out of her mind? By now Sam Cuccio was howling.

"Is anything wrong?" Melissa asked.

"No."

Luckily, she turned to Joey and they began speaking in tongues. Peter kept smiling. Pot pies consumed, he and Joey brought in dessert and coffee. A brick of three-flavored ice cream in a wet cardboard box, with a big spoon stuck in the middle. Now Rhoda would also know that we ate ice cream straight out of the container. Three flavors. But it no longer mattered. We polished it off in record time.

"That was delicious," Melissa said. As if they had just heard an intro to their dance number, Peter and Joey immediately rose again. They cleared the dishes together and both trotted off to the kitchen. Melissa and I were left at the table, listening to the sounds of things being scraped and dumped. Water ran. The back door opened and closed, indicating garbage had been disposed of. Then there were more clean up noises from the kitchen.

Melissa smiled at me knowingly.

"Right on!" she piped, making a V with her tiny fingers.

"I beg your pardon?"

"You've certainly got those two whipped into shape."

"Whipped into shape?"

"Men are such shits," Melissa said with relish.

Where had I heard this before? "No, really I can't agree with that. I—"

Disappointment narrowed the blue eye not covered by the great mop of Melissa's hair. "My mother said you were a great feminist."

"I am, but—"

"Then, come on, Lish," Melissa said. Lish? What had happened to

Mrs. Lasker? "You know that men are the enemy."

Yes, indeed she sounded like a mini-me. A mini-Charlotte. I wanted to explain that you had to earn such opinions, fight on the barricades, put your money where... But just then my two enemies came back, wiping their hands on dishtowels. Peter tossed his aside and went off to his study. Joey looked at Melissa, beaming. Joey, stop beaming. This girl wants to cut your balls off. How could I tell him that? Should I even want to tell him that? Oh, this metaphoric daughter business was more complicated than I figured. Even more than metaphoric sisters of the movement.

I remained for a while at the diningroom table, after everyone had left it, finding it hard to believe that this was the same place where I worked in the daytime. I put my typewriter and manuscript back in the middle to reestablish residence, but it still didn't look convincing. Then I went down the hall to Peter's study.

Here there were no signs of domesticity, only of a pure male professorial presence. Books were piled everywhere, including on the studio couch, where Peter was sitting. There was a real desk with a big office typewrite on it, mounds of paper, and blue books. Peter was deep in a sheaf of exams when I walked in, but shoved some books off the couch so that I could sit down.

I had come in, I thought, to talk about Joey, but what was there to discuss, really? His upbringing had been largely left to me. As to sex, the thought of it in connection with Joey made me prickly all over. I knew that some day soon I'd have to get over that—Joey's voice was changing, for God's sake—maybe finally put Peter in charge. But for now, I knew that if I even criticized Melissa, I would only sound like a mother-in-law. Peter's mother-in-law, unfortunately.

I lingered for a while, anyway, realizing that Peter hadn't shoved that many books and manuscripts off the couch after all. I was still surrounded by them, even more than usual. "What's all this stuff?" I asked, pointing to what wasn't on the floor.

VANITY FARE

"Submissions for the Maxwell prize."

"So many? So soon?"

Not that it mattered to me personally. No, the unwritten but binding Columbia nepotism laws would be at work here too, even if I ever could write something worthy, which was doubtful, particularly the way things were going. But then again, the joke was that a famous, successful writer like Charlotte Burns was no more in the running than I was.

I leafed through a volume or two from the piles surrounding me—they were either huge or very slim—and dropped them again. "Oh, well, I suppose now you'll never have time to read Vanity Fare."

"I have read it," Peter said.

"I meant Charlotte Burns, not Thackeray."

"I know."

"Really? Where did you get hold of it?"

"In our living room, on the middle bookshelf," Peter said.

Where I had proudly put it, all autographed.

"And?" I asked, battening my hatches against something along the lines of too commercial.

"Commercial to be sure," Peter said. Aha! "But better than I thought it would be. It's interesting that the comic treatment of small domestic matters owes its resonance to certain Victorians, not least, Mrs. Gaskell."

As usual, when there was literary content involved, my husband had lapsed into academic forked tongue and went on for a bit.

"You ought to write and tell that to Charlotte," I said. "The part about Mrs Gaskell." I knew she'd be pleased to hear it, if amazed.

"Okay," Peter agreed.

"She's working on another one, you know."

Peter nodded absently. But I had lost him. He was back in the land of the Maxwell Prize, where Charlotte and I had no place.

Later on, getting ready for bed, I took the Bergdorf shopping bag out of the closet. I knew I would return the dress. It had only been a moment of madness. But since I was standing around in my underwear anyway, I decided to try it one last time, take my own personal snapshot of me in it before I returned to reality and got my money back. I wrenched it down over my hips, then attempted to wrench it back up over my bosom. Could I have gained weight since this afternoon? My bra straps had somehow straggled into the picture. I shoved them out of the way, stepped back from the mirror, turned sideways. I suddenly saw Peter behind me in his light blue pajamas, just emerging from the bathroom. He stopped dead.

"Wow!" Peter said.
"I know, I know. Don't worry. I'm returning it."
"Returning it? What for?"
"Well, look how low it's cut, for God's sake."
"I am looking."
"Anyhow, where would I wear it?"

This was not the kind of question Peter usually took an interest in, though he was gazing at me thoughtfully. Too thoughtfully.

"No, Peter," I said. "Not now."
"Oh, come on," he said, smiling.

How could I get out of this? Should I tell him that I had a headache? That I had overdosed on tea and petit fours at the Plaza? But I had never wanted to "get out of this" before. Next thing I'd be lying there worried about my canning. Peter was sliding the thin straps off my shoulders—it was just like a man to admire something for the sole purpose of taking it off. Now he was nuzzling my cleavage. Looking down at his shiny blond hair, I felt that I had already betrayed him. "Oh, Peter."

"What?"
"Nothing."

He seemed to believe me, which was disconcerting. He kicked the door shut and led me to bed. Then the two of us were entangled in the act of love. It was familiar, safe, warm. I felt as I always did when

VANITY FARE

Peter came into me, made whole. Afterwards I lay nestled in my husband's arms, an emotional homing pigeon until I saw the Bergdorf dress lying rumpled on the floor. I would never be able to return it now. Ironic that this souvenir of guilty passion would now take up cozy, domestic residence in my closet.

Peter began to rummage for his pajama pants under the sheet, fair hair sweetly rumpled. I thought of all those Jewish writers, like Milton Gottlieb, David Harvey, Philip Roth, and their pursuit of the cool blond shikse whom they then proceeded to destroy. Could Peter be my male version? Of course not. He was Jewish too, though he didn't look it. But I had scared myself.

"Oh, Peter," I said passionately. "I love you. I love you. No matter what happens you'll always believe that, won't you?"

Peter laughed. "What movie is that from?" Peter said.

That night I dreamed a blue streak. Not in itself surprising. Dreams had always been important to my life—my first novel was called Classnotes of a Dreamer, after all, and I was even kind of famous for my dreams locally. Peter liked to hear them in the morning, and even Edward Maxwell had called them, approvingly, fruits of the fictive imagination. In my dreams I had written long, baroque, perfectly constructed periodic sentences worthy of Henry James, held meaningful conversations with my dead father about my mother, had tea with Elizabeth and Philip at Buckingham Palace (they were a surprisingly nice couple, with lovely accents, and it seemed rude to ask her what the hell was in that pocketbook she always carried around), conceived plots for murder mysteries, had an incredibly torrid encounter with JFK in the Lincoln bedroom while Marilyn Monroe and Jackie looked on, their mouths large O's. That night, however, I was looking down at Joey in his crib. He was contentedly sucking on his bottle. I shook a silver rattle. He dropped the bottle to reach for it, vainly, and started to bawl. When I woke up, I was in a panic, my fists clutching empty air.

"What was it this time?" Peter asked interestedly, the next morning at breakfast.

A veteran of my nocturnal habits, he was practically a partner in them. In fact, once, when he had done something bad in my dream, I had demanded he wake up and apologize. Which he did.

"Oh, nothing," I said. "Just a run of the mill nightmare. Not worth telling about."

"'I could be bounded by a nutshell,'" Peter quoted, in between bites of scrambled egg, "'and count myself a king of infinite space, were it not that I have bad dreams.'"

"But why can't that line be interpreted another way?" I said.

"What do you mean?"

"I mean, why can't Shakespeare be saying that Hamlet would be stupidly smug if his dreams didn't nudge him out of it?...After all, what's the hell's so great about being bounded by a nutshell?"

"Lish," Peter said firmly. "You're missing the point."

Why was I so sure Sam Cuccio would have understood?

No, there was nothing else for it. After tossing and turning a few more days, I called Charlotte. I hadn't heard from her in a while, which wasn't surprising. I knew she was busy and important. Another time I might have been hurt, anyway, about being ignored, or at least felt shy about intruding. But this was not the moment to stand on ceremony. Sam Cuccio was too hot a topic to ignore—dreams were piling up—and I needed expert advice. Charlotte was, after all, the only one I knew who knew him. But to my astonishment, though I called at the usual time, a decent interval after breakfast, it was her husband Steve who answered.

"She's not here, Lish," Steve said, in a portentous male voice. Had she left him? Was that it? Become totally fed up at last?

"Well, where is she?" I said boldly. "I'd like to talk to her."

"You can't talk to her now," he said, waiting a moment after my shocked silence to add, "she's in the hospital."

VANITY FARE

"Hospital? My god, Steve, what happened?"
"She had an operation. But it's okay. Everything turned out okay."
"Really? But can I see her?"
Steve hesitated. "She doesn't want any visitors, Lish. I'll tell her you called."
"Please do that."

I put down the phone, realizing that I didn't know where to call Charlotte on my own, and that Steve hadn't volunteered any information on that score. His diffidence was puzzling. It sounded like cancer, or something else terrible. But Steve had said she was okay, and he was an MD, after all, though a psychiatrist, and I didn't think he'd lie about that. Still, I was worried.

A week or so later, Peter and Joey had just left on their own morning rounds when the phone rang. For one frantic moment, I thought it was Sam Cuccio, and became hysterical. I told myself not to pick up, that he was just toying with me, a booze hound and bounder. That I was an idiot to have fallen for his cheap womanizing tricks when I knew the man's reputation. I picked up the phone anyway, my heart still pounding wildly even after I realized it was Charlotte on the other end.

"Oh, Charlotte!" I said, pausing to catching my breath, guilty because I had almost forgotten all about her. "Are you okay? Are you home? Steve said you were sick but not to visit."

"I'm still in the hospital, sweetie," Charlotte said in a weakish voice. "Where I'm afraid I'll remain until somebody gets me out of here. My very conservative doctor insists that—"

"Do you want me to come and spring you, is that it?"
"Oh, Lish, could you? Would you?"
"Of course, but—"

"Steven has to see patients until evening," Charlotte said, answering my unasked question. "But if I don't get out of here right now I'll go mad."

It seemed to me that Steve could certainly have cancelled a few analytic sessions under the circumstances. Didn't he realize that his wife needed him as much as his patients did? But I said nothing to Charlotte except that I'd get dressed and be right over. Still it gave me yet another unhappy insight into her marriage.

Doctor's General was exactly the kind of hospital I'd have expected to find Charlotte in. Very posh and very private on a tree-lined street on the Upper East Side. Not that this really mattered, since all hospitals scared the hell out of me, and I'd always felt that anybody who walked into one, including visitors, had maybe a fifty-fifty chance of walking out again. Nevertheless, I was the person Charlotte had turned to in her hour of need, not one of her older friends like gap-toothed AC/DC Nancy Tarkov. Personally I wouldn't have turned to Nancy Tarkov, either, but it still seemed like some kind of honor that Charlotte had chosen me. It reinforced the idea that everything I felt about her she felt about me too.

So I steeled myself against the fraught medicinal smells inside, and ultimately found Charlotte on a floor that had patients shuffling up and down in their bathrobes, lugging along their bottles and lifelines. A cruel setting for fastidious Charlotte, who was standing alone and fully dressed in her room. A departing red-haired nurse gave her a peculiar, hostile look as I entered.

"You look great, great," I said to Charlotte, babbling away in my nervousness. In fact she looked pale and lousy. "Wonderful. Let's get out of here."

Uncharacteristically discreet, I didn't ask her anything about her illness. I'd wait until she wanted to tell me on her own.

"Thanks, Lish," Charlotte said, touching my arm. Under the circumstances, I wasn't sure whether she was grateful for my coming or my shutting up. Actually, she really didn't look too bad. Wan, and with too much red lipstick, a few thin lines running up from it at the sides of her mouth. But beautifully put together in beige slacks and a tailored silk beige blouse, and a plaid-lined Burberry raincoat casually thrown over them. Her hair was held back with a brown grosgrain bow. Yes, the woman had pride and style. Still, I realized that she must also be very weak. I offered her my arm, but she refused it with a smiling shake of her head. She did let me carry her overnight bag, though, as we went back down the hall, and picked up some forms, handed to us by the hostile nurse.

"What is your relationship to the patient?" the nurse asked dubiously.

"Sister," I said.

Charlotte smiled at the feminist buzzword. But I meant it.

Outside, when we were safely settled into a taxi, I said,"Boy, that nurse is some care giver."

Charlotte had put on a kerchief and sunglasses, which made her look like an incognito movie star. "Well, isn't that always the way female illness is treated?"

"I guess."

"Though I'm afraid, sweetie, I made a few scenes."

"A few scenes?"

"On account of being subjected to a hysterectomy. Which I didn't want."

"A hysterectomy. Oh, God. Did they really think it was necessary?"

"They did. I didn't. Steven, of course, was on their side."

So this explained Steve's reticence as well as his absence. Explained, but hardly excused. Charlotte was right. More and more it was coming clear that women's bodies were constantly being violated by male doctors. Breasts lopped off, ovaries scooped out. (Hadn't Nancy Tarkov done an article for Ms. on the subject? Again, I was moved that nevertheless Charlotte had asked me for help, not her.) And now Charlotte's own husband had sided with the violators, in spite of her protests. No wonder she thought all husbands were bastards. I turned and saw her wince as we drove over a pothole. My heart went out to her. She gamely straightened up and smiled at me. But below the kerchief and sunglasses her skin was very white, her lipstick redder.

"Well, at least now I definitely don't have to worry about getting knocked up," she said, jokingly.

The joke was as weak as Charlotte, she was so clearly long past childbearing age. Still, in spite of all my own real fears about getting pregnant again—I wasn't kidding when I told Joey it was either being an only child or an orphan—I didn't delude myself that it wouldn't be awful anyway, having it all taken out, finished, kaput. A death knell for one's essential womanhood, or what we had been taught was our essential womanhood.

"Oh, Charlotte," I said, patting her hand. I didn't know what else to do, except roll down the taxi window and try to let in a bit of the faint spring air. Yes, true spring was finally on the way. We were going up Park Avenue toward her house. Slender budding trees stood outside elegant apartment buildings. The traffic islands in between swayed with the green bobbing heads of newly planted tulips that hadn't opened yet. Here and there a tiny yellow crocus showed its head. It was all beautifully promising.

"Summer will be here before we know it," I said, hoping to sound cheerful. "Do you have any special plans?"

Charlotte sighed. "The Hamptons again, I suppose. We have a house there, you know. A ghastly house. Pseudo colonial, and another pain in the ass to take care of."

"Why don't you sell it, then?"

"Steven loves it."

"Oh."

Another nail in the coffin of their marriage. Why didn't she just bust out of it, then? But at Charlotte's age it wouldn't be so easy. It wouldn't be so easy at mine, either, I hastened to tell myself. Not that I wanted to. I hastened to tell myself that also.

"So what's new, darling?" Charlotte said, changing the subject. "I seem to have been out of touch with the outside world for ages."

"The world? Oh, well, it seems to be going to hell in a handbasket, as usual. Patty Hearst says she's joining up with the nut cases who kidnapped her. She looks kind of cute in her beret, though. There's not too much hope for the ERA. Norman Mailer—"

"—and in your own life? Steven said you sounded as if you had something urgent to tell me."

"Urgent? No. Absolutely not."

"Lish, dear, he's a psychiatrist. Recognizing urgent is his specialty," Charlotte said, laughing. "What is it? Tell me."

Well, it was hardly the time or place, but she was insisting. And maybe she could use a little diversion.

"Okay," I said. "It's a man."

I expected her to laugh again, ask his name, come up with giggly, intimate questions. But she said quietly, "Is it serious?"

"Of course not. Nothing's happened yet. Nothing's going to. I'm just temporarily obsessed. It's okay. I've been obsessed before. I'll get over it."

"Would I know him?"

"I'm afraid so." I took a breath. "It's Sam Cuccio."

"Oh, my God!" Charlotte said. "Sweetie, he's very bad news."

But hadn't she once suggested that Sam was harmless? Why was she going out of her way to play hardball on this? I doubted she had trodden the straight and narrow all her married life. And furthermore, Vanity Fare, her own book, was full of passages about seizing the moment, etc. She could obviously tell from my face that I was annoyed.

"I'm sorry, sweetie. That was out of bounds. All that dopey medication must still be wearing off. Tell me about it. Really, I'm dying to hear."

"There's nothing to tell."

"I said I was sorry."

So I told her about it, as much as I knew, which was damn little. "...And that's where it's at," I concluded. "Which is to say, nowhere."

"Leave it there, Lish," Charlotte said, with surprising urgency. "Leave it there."

We had arrived at her apartment building. A doorman grandly reached into the taxi and took Charlotte's overnight bag as if she were returning from a trip abroad. Then he extended his arm to help her out. I tried to follow her, but she shook her head.

"No, darling, I'll manage. But thanks for your help, Lish. Really, thanks." I gingerly hugged her goodbye, knowing she must be in pain, afraid to hurt her more.

She smiled at me, adjusted her movie star scarf and dark glasses, then started to follow the doorman inside, very dignified, and very much alone. Steve should have been there, Steve should have come for her. I knew she didn't want him to, but he should have been there anyway.

"Oh, and Lish?" Charlotte turned.

"Yes?"

"That other matter." She smiled again. "Don't risk it. Please. Trust me on this one."

"All right, I will," I said, watching the doors finally close after her.

Of course. She had probably had an affair with him herself, which had ended badly. And so it was amazing that even in the midst of all her troubles, her illness, her memories, Charlotte could be so passionate, so caring about me. God, I admired the woman. No, I loved her.

II

4

Charlotte's life in East Hampton was as impressive as I had imagined. In the town, an exciting local literary scene, with pubs and restaurants where famous writers were regulars. On the beach, groups of them stood around, drinking and chatting away as if they were at a cocktail party. And here on Charlotte's own turf, except for the faux Colonial house which reflected Steven's taste, anyway, everything else was exactly what the home of a celebrated author ought to have been. Beautiful furnishings, beautifully landscaped grounds, the gorgeous pool, which I was happily heading toward now, wrapping myself, or trying to wrap myself, in the skimpy beach towel I had brought from home. I was joined by Charlotte, who naturally was wearing a long glamorous white terry cloth robe. We were intercepted by Steve. He stood up from his lawn chair, and put down the copy of the Times he had been reading.

"Are you going swimming again?" he asked Charlotte, with a worried frown.

"Obviously," she said, moving on.

"Don't stay in too long, this time. Don't overdo."

"Do I ever?"

"Look, Charlotte, you're still convalescing. I don't think you realize how serious an operation it is."

"Even though it was unnecessary?" she asked, stopping in her tracks, and turning to him. "Even though I was forced into it?"

Steven's solicitous smile faded and became something else.

"Oh, well, darling," he said, "at least now you don't have to worry about getting knocked up."

"That's not funny, Steven," Charlotte said.

"It wasn't funny when you were, my swan."

Both of them had forgotten I was there. Charlotte had forgotten she had made the same bad joke to me. Shrugging, Steven sank back into his chair with the Times, and immersed himself in the latest Watergate news, as if that were the only betrayal that mattered. I was almost touched by him. He had meant to be kind and caring, at least initially, and she had cut him off. But he hadn't needed to be so snide in return, so knowing, so terribly cutting himself. The Jewish doctor as God. I could see where it would drive Charlotte nuts. But she said nothing.

We continued on to the pool, where I immediately gave up my struggle with the beach towel and submerged myself in the water, glad that I and my black tank suit, advertised as sleek and slenderizing, which it wasn't, would be quickly hidden from view. Charlotte remained standing at the pool side, still wrapped in her long terry cloth robe, and smiled down at me.

"Aren't you coming in?" I called.

"In a bit. Go ahead."

I fooled around, did a couple of lengths, floated on my back, bobbed up and down, waiting for her to join me. I guess what I had in mind was two girlfriends dallying, laughing and chatting in the water. But Charlotte clearly wanted none of it. I finally came out, and picked up the towel again, wet hair dripping down my neck. Charlotte, meanwhile, sheathed in her long white robe, stood like a Greek statue, impervious to the elements. Until, that is, she surprised me by suddenly putting on two bathing caps, one over the other, and huge swimming goggles. Taking off the terry robe, she left for last. Underneath she wore a blue swim suit with a little skirt, and she was certainly thin enough for it, but in the bright sunlight her bare arms seemed a bit slack and crepey. She quickly dove into the pool. Not, as I had, because she was wished to conceal herself. That was hardly Charlotte's style. But as if she needed the freedom of the water, as if once submerged in that pool she would be in her element. And she was. Whipping through the water, she looked beautiful, slender, slippery, eely. Back and forth from one end of the pool to the other, back and forth steadily, she went, melting into the water, almost melting away. After a while, though, I became frightened watching her. Would she never come out? The phrase "Fear death by water," came into my mind. T.S. Eliot...But Virginia Woolf had weighted her pockets with stones, and waded straight in until she sank. Did she welcome the water rising slowly above her head?..."For I have heard the mermaids singing, each to each. I do not know if they will sing to me."...T.S. Eliot again....Crazy thoughts. Where had they come from? I was only watching Charlotte do laps.

When she came out Charlotte looked at me peculiarly. She quickly wrapped herself in the terry cloth robe and went toward the faux Colonial house.

The furniture in the living room was all white, sofas, deep covered arm chairs, curtains airily floating in the sea breeze, French doors opening onto a patio. No sign of Steven's taste here. This time I thought of The Great Gatsby, and the wonderful scene where Daisy and her friend Jordan, also in white, are idly lolling on a summer's day. The epitome of the idle rich, the jaded idle rich. I myself was sitting on a white sofa too, but as unrich and unjaded as it was possible to be, awaiting the imminent dinner party in a long black cotton skirt that tended to bunch up, and a straining white ruffly blouse. Charlotte, svelte in silky print evening pajamas sat down next to me. "Sweetie," she said, taking my hand, "your cheeks are flushed."

"It's only the sun."

"I hope you're not flushed with excitement or anything like that," she said, laughing. "Because, as I told you, the guests are only the usual suspects. Hampton regulars."

As if to prove her point, the first guest walked in. Herb Lobel, wreathed in smiles, as always.

"Thank God, he didn't bring one of his insufferable bimbos," Charlotte murmured. "I asked him not to. But whatever I say he always looks at me as if he were in his professional capacity. Don't you find that too, sweetie?" She rose to greet him.

Peter had already joined Herb. Peter was also smiling. But on Peter, handsome in his light blue summer jacket, the smile looked good. Soon the others drifted in too. Charlotte had filled me in on them in advance. Karl Brach, the director of her movie, whom I had met at her New York party. Arlene Mott, the editor, who had left her husband for Nancy Tarkov, who had in turn left Arlene. Charlotte said she herself had met Nancy Tarkov when Nancy wrote a very favorable review of Vanity Fare for the Times Book Review. The beginning of Nancy's feminist period, though Charlotte doubted it would last, there had been so many other periods before that, including a flirtation with Catholicism. Charlotte had concluded her guest list with a rueful shake of her head. "Oh, sweetie, I know what you're thinking. Four men and four women. Not that I really care about such things as balancing tables. It's just my old Noah's ark training." She smiled wearily. "But the truth is the social world still comes two by two." Maybe hers did. Mind didn't come as anything. I didn't give posh dinner parties, much less balance them.

Steven was now going about, offering me and everyone else a drink. I accepted a gin and tonic and stood up to join the group,. Soon the room was full of light chatter. The regulars were in their summer modes, tanned and hectic looking. I watched Charlotte go off to the kitchen, to check on the meal, I supposed. But in a few minutes she emerged, pulling her daughter Cynthia by the hand.

"You don't have to change, darling," Charlotte told her. "The jeans will be fine. Well, maybe an unfrayed pair, and a clean top. We're all friends here. You know everyone."

"Oh, Mother," Cynthia said, clearly distressed.

"Darling, I'm not going to eat you," Charlotte said. And let Cynthia slip back through the kitchen door. She looked after her, then invited us all into the dining room.

VANITY FARE

It was a cold, elegant dinner. Platters of beautiful things were waiting on the buffet. We all sat down at a long glass oval table, our chair seats covered with a wild purple print that was repeated in the place mats. I was amazed by the boldness of the pattern, especially after the whitest white of the livingroom. It was as surprising as Charlotte's bright red fingernails. Maybe it was her private homage to some wild summers of the past. I knew I would never ask her, and not about the fingernails either and so I gave my attention to the cold moules ravigotes, a plate of which waited at each place, impressive in itself. Peter was at Charlotte's right, Arlene next to him, Herb Lobel next to her. On Steven's right I was seated between Karl Brach and Nancy Tarkov, who palpably disliked each other. Being in the middle of this sandwich wasn't my idea of heaven. But I guessed that Charlotte hadn't wanted to seat Nancy Tarkov too near Arlene Mott, even though according to Charlotte their history was definitely history.

Nancy again started to urge me to join her professional women's organization, when Karl Brach interjected, "You're worried about such crap when the whole constitution of the United States is being subverted?"

"Women are always asked to take a back seat to 'more important events,' Nancy said, smiling her complacent gap-toothed smile. "It's time you realized we are the important events. Conspiracies in Washington will merely come and go, I assure you."

"You're a political idiot," Karl said.

Probably true. But he didn't have to put it that way. Which didn't stop Nancy from turning again to me. I smiled uneasily and then dug into a sublime vitello tonnato, a dish I had never seen outside of a restaurant and which Charlotte had served up from the buffet table along with a tomato and arugula salad and a perfectly ripened brie.

"Oh, Charlotte, this is all so gorgeous," I said. "Did you make it yourself?"

"Of course not, sweetie."

Next to me, Steven raised an eyebrow. At me, I supposed, and my foolish question. Because, among other things, this was just the kind of culinary triumph that Charlotte's heroine constantly struggled to achieve in Vanity Fare and that Charlotte had satirized so brilliantly. But with a touch of kindness too—which was what made it such a great book. "We were all in one way or another Donna Reeds in our day," I remembered her saying in an interview. "If we weren't, what would have been the need for the women's movement?"

"And what do you do, if anything?" Karl Brach asked me, abandoning Nancy Tarkov, probably permanently.

"Well, I'm a writer," I said, realizing that as usual I sounded as if I were lying. "A novelist actually," I added, with a glance at Charlotte, who smiled encouragingly.

"Oh? Would I have read anything you've written?"

"For god's sake, Karl," Charlotte said, "how the hell would she know what you've read?"

"Who's your publisher?" Arlene asked, briefly interested.

"Crutchworth did the last one. The first one. The only one."

"Oh," Arlene said, and turned back to Peter, to whom she'd been talking all along, telling him about the important and serious writers whom she edited at Colophon Press.

"I don't think I ever thanked you properly for your wonderful letter," Charlotte said to him, when there was a pause.

"Well, Vanity Fare's a wonderful book," he said charmingly, possibly glad of the distraction.

"Maybe," Charlotte said. "It's kind of you to suggest that. But truly, it's so heartening and gratifying—and rare—to have one's work treated to criticism of such a high level. Real literary criticism."

In fact, his letter, which I had read, had been all academic goobledygook, but sweet. Relieved to be on familiar ground, Peter launched into more of the same. Mrs. Gaskell kept coming into it somehow. Really, he was adorable.

Steven went into the kitchen to get dessert—raspberries under a light creme chantilly, lace cookies on the side—and came back with a still extremely shy Cynthia. She was sadly pale among us tanned adults. (But she was an adult too, I suddenly realized.)

"Cindy," Steven said with a bright smile, "say hello to our friends."

Which was exactly what she said. "Hello." However, in an obvious effort to please her mother and spruce up for those friends, she had changed her outfit, and now wore a white summer dress and a black velvet hairband, which still didn't look right because her bare feet were in the same unlaced old dirty running shoes. Charlotte visibly winced. My heart went out to her. Because really the girl could have been quite beautiful. I caught Herb Lobel giving Cynthia his terrible clinical smile.

Cynthia was allowed to depart. Followed by silence. Followed by Steven asking me, "Do you have children?"

"One. A boy," I said, smiling.

"Joey," Peter said, smiling too. We were a couple again. "He's at camp for the month. A junior counselor."

"Does he like it?" Steven asked.

"Not really, but he decided he's too old to spend a whole summer with his parents," I said laughing.

My laugh ended embarrassedly. It had struck me that much older Cindy was spending the summer with her parents. Another silence.

"Actually, I miss him," I said.

Steven stood up, offering cigars, which the other men, including Peter, surprisingly, accepted. It was obviously some kind of male bonding ritual. Since Charlotte had made clear she detested the smell, he led them out to the patio to smoke them. Charlotte wasn't too crazy about the patio, either, which Steven was planning to enlarge. "Pure suburbia." Of course she understood why. It was all the daydream of a once poor city boy now self-made, she had told me. Like so many things in their lives, which she didn't give a damn about, like the Blackgama mink coat he had foisted on her. Foisted on her? I couldn't imagine being so indifferent to a gorgeous mink coat, even if the life of the mind was uppermost. But Charlotte meant it. I had seen her throw that mink on irritably, like an old rain coat, that first night after Herb Lobel's party. On the other hand, what did I know about the exalted spheres, financial and literary, in which Charlotte lived?

The men departed, we ladies wandered back into the living room. I almost expected Charlotte to ask us if we wished to powder our noses. I sat back down on the white Great Gatsby couch. And Charlotte again sank down beside me. Nancy and Arlene had each taken positions on opposite sides of the room, Nancy outlined against the white wall in an unfortunate outfit involving red hot pants, Arlene in some kind of flowered Lily Pulitzer mumu.

"Are you sure I can't help clean up?" I asked, in the conversational lull.

"No, sweetie, thanks. Someone will come in."

"You're sure?"

"Positive, sweetie."

I pulled at my long skirt, which was bunching up again around my middle. "How do you keep so thin with dinners like that? I'm stuffed. It was really great, though."

"Steven loves dinner parties," Charlotte said.

"I guess men don't realize how much time and effort they take," I said. "But maybe I ought to start giving them too."

"No. Why should you?"

I couldn't think of a reason. Arlene Mott was quietly observing us from the other side of the room. But Nancy Tarkov in her hot pants had drifted out to the patio to join the men. It was night now, and Steven had turned on the outside light. Through the French widows they were all grouped together as on a stage set. Nancy was flirting with all the men simultaneously, her head, with its bush of kinky black hair, turning from side to side, coquettishly—she thought. It was pitiful how she strained to attract attention. The men all looked unhappy, not least Karl Brach, whose remarks she seemed to have forgiven, but who was clearly still disgusted with her. Only Peter looked sympathetic, as usual kindly inclined toward what he took to be a lady in distress.

VANITY FARE

"Anyhow, it's being a wonderful weekend," I said with a happy sigh. "I can't thank you enough. And that pool—you're a terrific swimmer."

"Oh, come on."

"I know. The pool was Steve's idea."

"Actually not. Steven was very much against my building one. He thought it was unnecessary with the ocean so nearby."

"But the ocean's different."

"I agree."

"Well, anyhow," I said, "I think it's heroic of you to have Peter and me here for the whole weekend. Especially since—" I stopped short, having almost wandered into the subject of her operation.

"Heroic? Hardly. No, it's wonderful to have you here. And impossible to get any work done in this damn house, anyhow."

I hesitated. "Look, Charlotte, I know that you've got Mort Glasgow as an editor, but if you—"

"I don't have Mort Glasgow anymore."

"You've left him?" I asked.

"Yes." She paused as if she were rejecting some explanation. "Anyhow, it's all water under the bridge, thank god. Over and done with."

"Well, then," I said hesitantly, "until you get a new editor, if you ever need—"

"I have a new editor," Charlotte said, smiling.

"Really? Who?"

She turned on a table lamp, and inclined her head across the room toward Arlene Mott, who regarded us silently. My mouth practically flew open. This dumpy expressionless woman in a dumpy flowered dress, her hair dyed so black, it could have been a fright wig? This was Charlotte's new editor? Charlotte smiled at me, as if she assumed I would understand. I didn't. But, again, what did I know about life on such exalted literary levels?

As we neared the city on the train, reality returned with a vengeance. Soot covered views of Queens lumbered past dirty windows. Sandwich wrappers littered the aisles. Children cried, passengers in shorts stuck to plastic seats. The kind of dismal Sunday night I remembered from high school, when the next day brought only tests and more homework, and a best girlfriend in braces. It was getting harder and harder to remember the shining, bleached landscape with its beautiful people we had left behind only a few hours, though it seemed ages, ago. It was even hard to keep Charlotte's white living room clean in my mind.

"You know, I've always had this idea that if I ever had a pool of my own, I'd be a better person. Not just physically, but morally too," I said to Peter. "Does that make any sense?"

"No."

The train jerked into a hot and airless station. Peter and I made our way underground into the worse inferno of the IRT subway in July, hit by the odor of greasy franks and sweaty bodies. As we rattled and shook in our subway seats going uptown, I tried to keep alive the small triumphs of the weekend. Karl Brach grandly inviting us all to the movie premiere of Vanity Fare in September. Peter being so handsome and self-assured that Charlotte had clearly liked him more and more. She had smiled at him with real enjoyment as they spoke together. Very hetero enjoyment, which had laid to rest any hasty thoughts about her and Arlene Mott. I'd never had a very good head for that stuff, anyway. It was even harder for me to imagine two women in bed together than Charlotte with her husband. Which wasn't to suggest that I didn't think Charlotte had been sexy in her day. Even now, beginning to show her age, she had a certain something about her.

I wondered why she had gotten rid of Mort Glasgow. I supposed she had merely tired of him. It must be marvelous to shuck off editors at will, acquire others for the mere asking, abandon publishers as you pleased. Someday, perhaps I too... And Peter, unlike Steve, would be staunchly at my side. True, he hadn't contributed anything when Karl Brach was asking about my work. But he could hardly blow whistles, ring bells in such sophisticated circles.

We got out of the subway at 116th Street and Broadway and, with Peter listing from the weight of our bags, walked the couple of blocks west to Claremont Avenue, deserted and joyless at the end of this summer weekend. The students gone, leaving behind only such local residents as the widow Maxwell and us. We would call Joey at camp the minute we got upstairs. Put on our one air conditioner, in the living room, full blast. Consider whether there was enough for dinner in the fridge or whether we ought go back downstairs again to a Broadway greasy spoon. Well, this is your life, Lish, I thought. For now.

The next day I really knuckled down to work and, maybe thanks to the heady inspiration of a weekend where successful writers lived, my book finally picked up steam. Reunion. Yes, a kind of sequel to Classnotes of a Dreamer, but more advanced, more mature. I had finally cracked my own literary puzzle, and the pieces were falling into place. Such as, what my characters did in bed, or at least what they said while they were doing it, in my case a major breakthrough. There was light at the end of the tunnel. And some of that old, remembered joy too. Charlotte always spoke of writing wryly, as if it were cruel and unusual punishment. I was ashamed to admit how much pleasure it could give me, even revision, which had such a bad reputation I wouldn't admit that to anyone. I could see eventually finishing my novel, and having it published. To the sound of one hand clapping, maybe—but published. I would no longer be a one book author, and that one a fluke. I sent the manuscript off to my toothy agent, Ramona, knowing it surely would require more work, and that it would be at least a week before she read it, several more before Crutchworth would deign to take another look. But I needed feedback.

Meanwhile, summer ended with a bang. Nixon resigned and flew off never to return, we hoped. In other areas—my own small areas—

the tide was turning too. To my amazement, I was invited to join the PEN Club, though two publised books were the usual requisite. To my further amazement I was soon also asked to join the membership committee. I laid this all at Charlotte's feet, certain she was behind it, though characteristically, even though she still called in the morning, first from East Hampton, then from New York, she never mentioned the matter. A great lady.

Yes, I'll do Charlotte proud, I decided, seated at the first PEN membership committee meeting of the season. (I was at a conference table with about ten other members including, to my dismay, Nancy Tarkov.) But when I dropped Charlotte's name, I was surprised to discover that Charlotte took no interest in PEN's activities at all.

"Maybe she thinks we won't help her sales," the pudgy poet who was our chairman said snidely.

"She doesn't think that way," I said, emboldened to speak up. "She's actually very shy. An extremely private person."

Nancy Tarkov smiled as if she were the one who had told me that in the first place. My confidence wavered, then faded totally when Sam Cuccio suddenly slid into a vacant chair across from me—about a half hour late. It had never occurred to me that he might belong to this committee too. Appointment in Samara. If I had known I would never have joined. No, stupid idea. Cowardly and unprofessional. But it was hard to be professional while Sam sat there grinning at me. (A souvenir from Charlotte's past?) I could only think how truly dark and handsome he was, even more dark and handsome than he had seemed at the Plaza. Also, his teeth were gorgeously white. Why hadn't I noticed that before?

"Did I miss anything?" Sam asked amiably.

"We were talking about getting Charlotte Burns to take a more active interest in PEN," I blurted out.

"Maybe you can persuade her," Sam said. He leaned forward across the conference table, giving me a heady whiff of what definitely wasn't tea. Probably that Lapsang Souchong at the Plaza was the only cup of tea Sam Cuccio had ever had in his life.

"I? Persuade her?" I said, leaning backward. "How?"

"You could tell her how much we do for freedom of speech. That kind of stuff."

"Well, she is very caring, of course," I said. "Very generous to other writers."

Again Nancy Tarkov smiled.

"There you are," Sam Cuccio said.

Everyone nodded, quietly impressed. Sam Cuccio kept grinning in my direction. Our superstar was now going public with his interest in me. I tried to shrug the whole thing off, but it wasn't easy. I had used the word obsession to Charlotte, and I hadn't exaggerated. Had the beautiful white teeth also put her over the top? No Jew, not even goyish looking Peter, had such teeth. They suggested pasta, lemon juice, sophistication, a capacity for intrigue. There was also that small, beguiling cleft in his chin, which I also hadn't noticed at the Plaza. Or had I? I reminded myself firmly that Charlotte had called him bad news. And that I had promised her not to take risks. She had exacted it like a deathbed promise. Still, in the end, the heroine of Vanity Fare had embraced carpe diem with a vengeance, which was why she had been such a heroine to me. A conundrum.

We sped through the rest of the business at hand. From my vantage point as an expert on the matter, and with Sam Cuccio nodding appreciatively, I nixed two professorial candidates who ground out academic nonsense—with silent apologies to Peter. The woman who wrote children's books made an impassioned plea that we include more children's book writers. "According to some literary critics, we too often have," Sam remarked pleasantly. Someone asked if we could invite Woodward and Bernstein jointly. What about Louis Auchincloss? Gore Vidal? Eudora Welty? (My suggestion) It turned out that these luminaries were already members or had turned us down. We would have to go farther afield. It began to get late.

Afternoon shadows shifted outside the uncomfortable and unpretty room where we sat, which was scantily furnished except for the old conference table and chairs, and the walls of floor to ceiling bookcases containing hundreds and hundreds of books by past and present PEN members. So many books, so many more to come, grains of sand sifting into the bottom of the barrel. Maybe I would make some such observation to Sam, who I was sure would agree. Maybe even ask joshingly if I thought his books were a few grains too many. The chairman announced the date for our next meeting, a month away, and the club secretary put away her notepad. I looked at Sam, who was looking at his wristwatch.

"Do you have time for a drink?" our pudgy poet/chairman said to me, sotto voce, as everyone else, including Sam Cuccio, got up to leave. The pudgy one took off his glasses and gazed at me with naked eyes.

"I'm afraid I must be getting on," I said hastily, but loud enough for Sam to hear. Whether he heard or not, I never learned. Because he was out the door by the time I got there, and Nancy Tarkov had presented herself confidently at my side.

"You never came to the professional women's group," Nancy said, as we proceeded along lower Fifth Avenue. "And here you've joined the PEN membership committee."

"Yes...well, since Charlotte nominated me, I—"

"You think Charlotte nominated you?"

She hadn't? No, this was just Nancy Tarkov's way of implying that whatever it was, she knew better than any one. I wished she hadn't attached herself to my side, never asking if I would welcome her company. She always made me nervous. I couldn't figure out what the hell she wanted of me, though whatever it was I wasn't interested. Now to make matters worse, she was smiling that gap toothed smile again. Maybe it wasn't fair, but I had always felt that people with gaps between their front teeth couldn't be trusted. Sneaky, stupid things could seep through. Look at the guy on the cover of Mad. I glanced around for a cab. It would be a hideously expensive ride from way downtown and I'd probably get caught in the rush hour, meter ticking. But I wanted to get away.

"Do you really think you can get Charlotte to take more of an active part in the organization?" Nancy asked, as cab after cab sped by.

"I have no idea. If she doesn't want to, I'm sure she has her reasons."

"Charlotte always has her reasons," Nancy said chillingly.

"What the hell does that mean?" I asked, not wanting an answer. Not from this woman. A cab finally stopped.

"See you at the next meeting," Nancy said. "I like you."

This time when I got home, my apartment felt like an oasis. Never mind that the furniture was more mix than match, that the sofa sagged in unexpected places, that in fact almost everything, despite Peter's tenure, remained Early Stipend. (Except for a small gilt table I had impulsively bought after that party at Charlotte's and that was already peeling.) The fact was that real, plain speaking people lived here, people without hidden agendas like that awful Nancy Tarkov. Even if she had once given Charlotte a great review, I didn't understand why Charlotte stuck with her.

Melissa was back again, and would doubtless stay for dinner. She had become a fixture in our house. Passing Joey's room, I saw him and Melissa sitting side by side on his studio couch, the picture of innocent contentment, though Joey looked more content than Melissa. He was clearly smitten, poor sot. How Melissa felt was less clear. She didn't repulse him, but indifferently let him sit with his arm around her, rubbing the sleeve of her t-shirt up and down.

I started to clear my stuff from the dining room table, wondering why Sam Cuccio had beat such a hasty exit out of the PEN Club. Would I ever understand that man? I put him aside, and tried to forget about Nancy Tarkov altogether. But what about Charlotte? If she hadn't proposed me for membership, who had? But I was just stalling. There was a message from Peter that my agent Ramona had called. If I called back now I would still get her at the office, but I wasn't sure I wanted to. No news might not be good news, but it wasn't bad news either. Well, maybe it was better to get the worst over with once and for all.

"Oh, Lish, dear..." My agent's voice, reproachful, high to the point of cracking, came over the wire.

Her tone made my heart seriously sink. I really couldn't deal with rejection at this moment. Maybe if I assured her I was willing to make changes?

"Changes?" Ramona said, dubiously. "Yes, but George Crutchworth seems to think—"

"He's read it already? Oh, my God, what did he say?"

"George is so odd," Ramona remarked cheerfully, "sometimes it's impossible to understand him. Let's see, where did I put my notes?"

"Never mind the exact wording," I said.

"No, wait a minute. I have them here somewhere. I had them out to read to you when Tessa Small popped in. Do you remember her, dear? I believe you were still working for me when I handled her first novel. Of course, in those days publishers were still pretending to be literary, unlike now, when it's all so hideously commercial. I always warn my young clients..."

I often wondered why my agent handled fiction at all since she had not the slightest idea of what a story was, much less how to tell one. She backed, she filed, made false starts and stops, wandered off into thickets. She was still lost, deep in the underbrush, when I allowed myself a brief respite. How lucky Charlotte was. Charlotte didn't even need to use an agent. Publishers ran after her, though why in God's name had she settled on Arlene Mott?

I tuned back in. "Goddamn it, Ramona!" I cried, unable to contain myself any longer. "What the hell did he say?"

"That's what I called to tell you, Lish, dear," she said, sweetly

surprised by my outburst. "He thinks it's a breakthrough."
"Breakthrough? What's a breakthrough?"
"Your book."
"My book's a breakthrough?"
We batted the concept back and forth several times—Ramona would have been content to go on forever—until I finally stopped her, and asked what it meant.
"Just that they all love it, and want to back it all the way."
"Back it all the way? What does that mean?"
"I don't know, I dear, but it can't be bad, can it?"
"No."
"He called it 'intelligent,'" Ramona added. "As I was saying to Tessa Small—"
I quietly hung up. Ramona would hardly know the difference.
But, oh, my God. I could barely take it all in. He loved my book. Crutchworth loved my book. They all loved my book. And intelligent! This was a new wrinkle. Last time out I had been "deft," sometimes "witty," on occasion "deft" and "witty." Intelligent augured well. I was being taken seriously. Of course, poetic would have been nice too, but you couldn't have everything.
"What's up, Ma?" Joey said, coming in, with Melissa behind him. "You look like you just swallowed a canary."
"Well, actually I was just talking to Ramona."
"And?"
"Crutchworth loves the new novel."
"You're kidding! That's great!"
"Ah," Melissa said, deeply impressed when Joey explained that I was talking about my agent and my publisher.
"He said I was intelligent," I added, unable to keep from wanting to impress her still further.
"Is it good for a novelist to be intelligent?" Melissa asked.
Good question. We stared at each other thoughtfully.
"Well, anyway," Joey said, breaking the ice. "Congratulations."

"It's too soon for congratulations, darling," I said superstitiously, wanting to ward off the evil eye. The two of them looked terribly disappointed, so I added, "Well, of course you're right about one thing. That first positive response is always important to a writer, because it means he, she, has finally come out in the open. Artistically speaking, so to speak. I mean if even one person gets what you mean, you haven't worked in vain. The whole solitary struggle finally has meaning. Do you know what I mean?"

There were too many "mean"s in that statement, but nevertheless I could feel my eyes grow misty. The two of them gazed upon me solemnly, sweet young faces on overgrown bodies. They were moved, I was moved. It was a moving moment. Peter had come in at the end of it, and stood there, discreetly not asking about dinner.

Afterwards, (Chinese take out), I had to call Charlotte. It wasn't our usual time, but I couldn't wait until morning. "...And oh, Charlotte, I know it must all seem like small potatoes to you—I mean George Crutchworth is hardly in the same league as your publishers—but I just had to tell you."

"I'm honored," Charlotte said, laughing. "Congratulations."

"It's too soon for congratulations," I began. No, I had gone that route before. "But I did want to thank you. Thank you for everything. Even if nothing comes of all this I already owe you so much."

"You owe me nothing," Charlotte said.

"Oh, I do! I do! You believed in me, you encouraged me, when all about me...Oh, shit... Excuse me... Never mind."

Charlotte did me the courtesy of hearing me flounder on to the end. Then high as a kite I drifted into the bedroom, where Peter lay on top of the spread watching the news on TV. I lay down beside him, and groped for his crotch. The entire day had fired me up. Creative juices were flowing all over the place. I was going to make final changes to that novel non-stop, whether Crutchworth wanted them or not. Peter turned to me with pleased surprise, as if he had worried that it would all go the other way, distract me from sex. For his sake, as well as mine, I almost wished it had.

5

This was nothing like the movie premieres of the old days, occasions of dazzling beauty and glamor, with stars emerging from limousines under bright klieg lights—beautifully gowned women dripping diamonds and white fox, escorted by gorgeous leading men in white tie and tails—as fans cheered in the bleachers. The stars would pause graciously to say a few words into the microphone for those at home. Cameramen would close in.

Tonight's premiere was held in an ordinary Third Avenue movie house, which had been closed to the public for a few evening hours. Steven and Charlotte were wedged in against the refreshment stand in the crowded lobby. Charlotte, cool and detached. Steven, a hale fellow-well-met, heartily shaking hands with whoever came by, waving the special souvenir program at others. People kept streaming in. Occasional celebrities, no doubt invited by Karl Brach, stuck up like pebbles. I recognized Paul Newman, Joanne Woodward, Arthur Penn, Madeline Kahn, Elliot Gould, and a few others less immediately recognizable, but familiar. Not that any of them were dressed like celebrities. There wasn't a white fox in the bunch, or silver fox, either, or dripping diamonds. No, they were all wearing the current uniform of "serious artists." Sweaters, jeans, leather jackets—Karl Brach included, though his jacket made him look pudgier. I guessed the Sixties were to blame, and in their case, Method acting too, which had helped eradicate glamor. It was really too bad. Why be stars if you couldn't look like stars? Or, for that matter, nuns either, who now wore drab mid-calf navy blue skirts and black oxfords. In her stunning off-white Chanel suit with crimson piping, pearls at her ears, Charlotte looked like the right word in the wrong context. Steven in his dark blue pin stripe completed the picture. I wondered if Charlotte had needed to talk him out of leather jacket and jeans. She would be comme il faut, no matter what. At that moment, she was reluctantly posing for the press with Karl Brach for pictures that would probably never run—"B-U-R-N-S," I heard her say repeatedly—until the photographers sped off to shoot the stars of the picture. The rest of us ultimately filed into the theater proper. I squeezed Peter's arm, then couldn't help turning around and giving Charlotte a little excited wave. Gauche, I knew. Pure hayseed. But I was very happy. And she didn't see me anyway.

We sat down, and presently the lights dimmed, always a moment fraught with anticipation. Then the lights went out completely, and the credits began, running over the opening sequence of a young woman entering a posh New York apartment house. Every name that flashed on the screen was the signal for private laughter, private applause. Finally there came, "Based on the novel by Charlotte Burns." More applause. Sporadic. No intimate laughter. She was a distinguished writer, after all, not one of the entertainment crowd. A sudden silence and then the movie took over, larger than life, more absorbing than life. Charlotte's book was lurking in there somewhere, but well hidden. The action was taking place in a "middle class" living room so posh that no middle class New Yorker could possible have afforded it. The female lead was a pretty little blonde who was supposed to be dark neurasthenic Margo, and the leering stud with the overstuffed crotch had been cast as her very urbane, sophisticated lover.

In a way it was all familiar, though at the same time it wasn't, since Charlotte had once casually asked if I wanted to visit the set and, surprised and flattered, I accepted eagerly. I'd never been on a movie set before. But it was far more tedious than I'd expected, even though Charlotte had warned me. They were doing the scene where Margo is seduced by Zack. I watched them do it over and over again. Take after take. A passionate embrace. Margo bent backward over the sofa by the ardent Zach, her housewifely hand reaching out to adjust a little something on the end table. Each time a voice yelled "Cut!"—or was that word left over in my mind from movie magazines?—the lovers broke apart, and it was like being doused in cold water. Suddenly the pretty little blonde was mousy, the gorgeous smiling hunk sullen. And then they were at it again. Gorgeous and handsome, wildly sexy. Amazing, this ability to go from passion to dispassion with the snap of a finger, a voice yelling "Cut!" Up on the screen, the filmed scene went by so seamlessly I could hardly fix it in my mind. There was a closeup of Margo trembling with terror and ecstasy. A closeup of her reaching hand. Explosive laughter. In the book the scene was meant to be funny. But this kind of funny? I'd never seen that reaching hand in closeup. Ultimately the movie was over and the credits rolled again. This time there was a long hush before the great burst of applause. The house lights went on while some of the audience was still clapping. A few overenthusiastic types had leaped to their feet to shout "Bravo!" "Vanity Fare"—(Karl Brach's "Vanity Fare")—was obviously a hit.

    The party at Sardi's, in a private room on the second floor, crowded only a few minutes ago, was emptying now. Most of the celebrities had already come and gone, whisked to and fro by limo—in this sense they were still every inch stars. There remained a scattering of minor lights, however, crying, "Darling!" And the usual tall wives towering over very short rich husbands—the current style in second marriages. Once more Steven and Charlotte were the object of congratulations, this time stationed near the bar, where Peter and I had just put down our empty glasses.

    "It's a hit, baby," Sam Cuccio said, coming up. He kissed Charlotte and went off, with a too familiar slap on her rump. Charlotte didn't react. Me, he seemed not to have noticed at all, which was just as well.

    "It is a hit, darling" Steven said to Charlotte. "I wish that made you happier."

"Oh, Steven, how can it? It's a second hand rendition of old work. There's nothing new here."

"Or under the sun, I suppose," Steven said, with a deep sigh, which for some reason he directed at us.

"It really is a wonderful film, Charlotte," Peter said.

"I'm glad you enjoyed it. Was it a film, though?" Charlotte laughed. "I though it was only a movie. In any case, I'm afraid I had nothing to do with it."

"You've had everything to do with it," Peter said, laughing too. "Movie or film it's still wonderful. And so is this party."

"Ah, but I've had nothing to do with this party, either," Charlotte said, but gave him a grateful little kiss on the cheek. It was sweet how much she liked him.

Nearby the two stars of Vanity Fare were standing together, looking dowdy as hell, and utterly bored.

"It's so fascinating," I said to Charlotte, observing them. "I kept thinking about that on the set. To see them so passionately in love, and to see them so totally not. What an incredible gift for illusion."

"It's all an illusion," Charlotte said. "They're both gay."

"Oh."

I stood there aimlessly, not sure why I was still standing there. I was hardly hoping to spot another celebrity. I nudged Peter. Maybe it was time to go home. We thanked Charlotte, and Steve too, for good measure, and were heading toward the door, when Karl Brach came walking straight toward me. Said a few astonishing words. And walked away again. My mouth hung open.

"Peter, he wants Ramona to send him my book!"

"I know. I just heard him."

"Maybe he says that to everyone."

"I doubt it."

I put my arm through his. "Oh, isn't this fabulous, though? I can't believe it's all happening to me. I mean, imagine having your book optioned for a movie. I mean even if he decides not to option it, just the idea is thrilling."

"Charlotte doesn't seem thrilled," he said, looking at her thoughtfully.

"Well, she's used to this kind of thing. Anyway, I'm thrilled."

"I'm glad," Peter said, with a perfunctory smile.

Peter often left my effusions unattended, so I decided not to let it bother me. Besides, movies had never meant much to him—with Peter it was books all the way. Still, he had meant it when he told Charlotte the evening was wonderful. And he looked great too, blond and handsome in his dark blazer, if a bit too academic for these surroundings, but thoroughly at ease nevertheless. I, of course, had hedged my bets, in basic black, boring basic black, not the Bergdorf number, and again envied Charlotte's immutable elegance, her perpetual soignee-hood, if that was a word.

When I saw Sam Cuccio moving in our direction, I stayed calm, telling myself that I was mistaken. But he, with his wife this time, was really coming over to us. For some reason Sam looked older than when I had seen him before, even when talking to Charlotte, swarthier, a touch sinister, though it was probably only the usual effect lots of famous people had of being sunburned out of season. His gleaming white teeth were revealed in a grin. (A wicked grin? No, even in connection with Sam, that was a cliche.) I presented Peter, ashamed to be so glad that he was presentable, and Sam introduced his wife. I had seen her briefly at Charlotte's party. A very new wife, from what I had read in the papers. In their wedding pictures, I now remembered, the bride was holding an infant. Young, too. I gave her a quick once over, actually not so quick because she was tall, willowy, and beautiful. She was wearing wide black satin pants, some kind of a draped shawl and stunning heavy silver earrings and bracelets. Peter wasn't short, I was. But for a moment there, a very unpleasant moment, I felt that we were both standing in a hole. I was afraid that Peter would say something enthusiastic, like, "I'm a great admirer of your work, Mr.

Cuccio." But he merely stood there good-naturedly, engaging in the usual ritual chitchat, until Sam and his wife drifted on.

Awful as the moment had been, I was sorry it had passed so quickly, especially when the next person who presented herself was Arlene Mott. I hadn't seen her since that weekend in the Hamptons. But my heart sank, the way it did when I was expecting something nice and my mother called from Florida. Dumpy Arlene's eyes regarded me coldly from under her black fright wig. I was glad her eyes were cold. I certainly wouldn't have wanted her to take a warm personal interest in me, though God knew I had done a lot of personal speculation about her. Repeat questions about how Charlotte could have left Mort Glasgow for this came into my mind. Then, for the first time, a glimmer of wondering if maybe Mort Glasgow had left Charlotte. No, impossible. Charlotte was too important an author, too well known.

"Great movie," I said finally, impelled by Arlene's silence to say something.

"The book is better."

"Yes, well…"

I was going to launch into my favorite theory about why good novels made bad movies and vice-versa, but remembered in time that I had just said Vanity Fare had made a good movie. At least I thought I had. Also, there was the fact that Karl Brach had just asked to see my book for a possible movie. Damn. Arlene, as usual, had poisoned all good feelings just by being there. Talking to her was like trying to find a comfortable place on a bed of nails. I looked at Peter, who stood pleasantly by my side. Then Arlene suddenly gave me a smile, a funereal one, but still a smile. It was unhinging, this sudden cordiality. She had never smiled at me before.

"Well, I haven't seen it yet, but I'm sure Charlotte's new book is great too," I said, babbling on.

"It is," Arlene said to Peter.

"I'm a great admirer of her work," I continued doggedly, and when this failed to impress added to my own horror, "...so's my husband."

"I know," Arlene said, again giving me that utterly chilling smile. Maybe Charlotte had passed the word to be nice, which would have been characteristic of Charlotte. Except that Arlene being nice was worse than when she was awful.

"Peter," I said, being wifely. "You have an early class tomorrow."

He nodded. Party lover though he was, he knew when duty called. I left him saying a last few words to Arlene and went to get my all-purpose trenchcoat (as much of a cop out as the basic black dress), which I had dropped on a chair when we came in. The souvenir program that I had stuffed into a pocket fell to the floor. I bent to pick it up, but a hand got there ahead of me. I rose to find myself looking into the dark eyes of Sam Cuccio. "I'll call you," he murmured, and while my mouth was still trying to work, walked away.

"Nice guy," Peter said, coming up from behind. "I'm a great admirer of his work."

"Well, I'm not," I said, which was true and confused me even further. So did Charlotte's expression from a distance, which I finally realized was only her familiar wry smile.

Ramona was now pleading for at least a piece of a third novel. Karl Brach's desire to see the last one had sent her hopes zooming into the stratosphere as well as fragmenting her train of thought beyond repair. I too was thrilled but, as usual, superstitious. Not sure I was getting through to her, I had asked Ramona not to mention the movie matter to anyone until we heard from Karl Brach again. For my own part, I hadn't even discussed it further with Peter. I had also not mentioned it to Charlotte. What was the point? She wasn't excited about her own book being made into a movie. All of which, for lack of anything better, created a vacuum immediately filled by the Cuccio obsession, an obsession that every time I merely laid eyes on the man appeared to come back full force. I didn't need a Herb Lobel to kindly tell me in shrink talk that I was being a major asshole in this connection, since

I knew perfectly well that in addition to all his other notorious faults, Sam Cuccio was a liar too. He had no intention of calling me, it was just something he said, like the check is in the mail. But why say it to me, when his wife was a gorgeous brunette who looked like a model? On the other hand…No, too many hands. My mind was beginning to resemble a troupe of Balinese dancers. Soon I would be in Ramona's league.

Okay. I couldn't help it. I had to talk to Charlotte about Sam again, the one person in my circles who knew him, though also the very person who had warned me against him. But that was the point. She had tried to cure me once, this time she would succeed. A wiser, older woman who had my best interests at heart. Not that I considered Charlotte motherly, a bad word in my vocabulary, anyway. In fact, Charlotte's maternal instincts seemed to be on the weak side, weaker than mine if the truth be told. But this made me trust her all the more.

"What's up, sweetie?" she asked cheerfully, when I finally took a deep breath and called one morning.

"Nothing," I heard myself say, not surprised that my good intentions had suddenly deserted me.

"Nothing?"

I stalled. "I mean, the movie got fabulous reviews, didn't it?"

"Did it? I haven't seen them."

"In the Times. Also Newsweek…"

"That's nice."

"You sound depressed, Charlotte, are you?"

"Not really."

No, remote was more like it. Obviously Charlotte had other fish to fry besides me and my idle phone calls, though she was doing her best to seem interested. A sobering thought. I should have worthier things on my mind too. She excused herself, explaining that she had to answer the doorbell, and then came back, saying that it was the new housekeeper and now she would have to follow her around and lose the morning. She really had to go. Unless there was something…?

"No, no. I understand. I won't keep you. But thanks again. I mean for the screening and the party and all."

"I'm glad you had that good a time," Charlotte said.

I hung up in a hurry, waves of guilt sweeping over me about being so man crazy, and also feeling that I had somehow violated our friendship. Not confiding in her about my obsession with Sam wasn't the same as withholding the news about Karl Brach. Of course, Charlotte kept things from me too. I understood that. But that was discretion. This felt like lying. Then on top of everything else there were Peter and Joey tiptoeing around the house all the time, like two conspirators. More guilt. I couldn't tell them I knew damn well my birthday was coming up and that I hated surprise parties.

Actually, none of it was a surprise until long after the party was underway and I saw Charlotte standing at the entrance to the living room, looking around.

"Oh, my God!" I cried, running over. "I didn't realize you were in on this too."

"I'm delighted to be here, sweetie," Charlotte said, looking around some more.

I'd laughingly described my apartment to her many times. Now she would see I wasn't kidding. Ahead of her, a dreary living room in what was often called "a great West Side apartment," but was actually a long corridor punctuated by other dreary rooms. The only real antiques being the plumbing.

"I haven't been up in this Columbia neighborhood for ages," Charlotte said. "Not since my college days."

"Really?"

"It's still rather monumental and grand, isn't it?"

"If you like faded grandeur."

"I guess it wasn't faded then. We'd come up to hear lectures and such. Also, Harlem was a very hot spot at the time, and—" She paused and laughed. "Well, no need to go into all that."

The pause brought to my mind black saxophonists beaded with sweat and other dark images that old time forays into Harlem were famous for. But there was nothing in the present cool and collected Charlotte to suggest any of it.

I led her into the living room.

"Listen, Charlotte," I said, sighing, "they're not my Ritz crackers."

"I beg your pardon?"

"And neither are those blobby things on top."

I was talking about the hors d'oeuvres that had been set out for the birthday party and were sitting about on soggy paper doilies.

"But, darling, if they're not yours, whose are they?"

"What I meant was that Peter and Joey thought it all up together. You see, they—"

"Oh, well, men," Charlotte said, smiling.

"Men," I repeated, trying to make myself smile too. Anyway, I thanked god she had come too late, probably purposely too late, for the cries of "Surprise!" and also for the cutting of the birthday cake, the remains of which sat on a side table surrounded by discarded pink candles and in close proximity to the Ritz crackers.

Charlotte handed me my gift. A large liquor bottle wrapped in gift paper.

"I'm sorry, sweetie, but I'm not very good at thinking up clever presents. Scotch. Twenty years old. To reassure you that certain things improve with age... God, that sounds awful. Who am I kidding?"

I took it gratefully. "Listen, everybody else brought gift soap. So what are they trying to tell me? Anyway, I .do apologize again for your being roped into this."

"Don't be ridiculous. Unfortunately, Steven—"

"I understand," I said, too quickly, putting the scotch on a side table.

I wanted to say that like the Ritz crackers, the guests weren't mine, either. But they were, including Rhoda Garfunkel, who was the first to come rushing over. Pretty and breathless, relentlessly cheerful, she

VANITY FARE

immediately informed Charlotte that she was an old Barnard classmate of mine.

Then, "I just love your book."

"How nice."

"Yes, Lish and I read and reread Vanity Fare many times in the old days. Well, Lish did. Actually, I only read it once. But it had a great effect on me too."

"Did it?"

"I was thrilled when she said she met you. I've always wondered why you've never written anything else since then. And now here you are. I'm thrilled."

"How nice."

I called Joey over, who was lurking nearby. "This is my son."

"I know. He took my coat."

At his side, like a limpet, was Melissa, whom Rhoda Garfunkel proudly identified as her daughter. The spitting image of her mother, and with a brain pan the same size. She too was thrilled to meet Charlotte, for some kind of obscure feminist reasons. Joey reserved comment. I could tell he didn't like Charlotte. I could also tell she didn't like him, either. Maybe he just seemed appallingly normal and uninteresting to her, a boy who, in the suburbs, would spend his life hanging out in the mall.

Then up came Ramona Brill, with her buck teeth and large eyeglasses, who began to speak at Charlotte nonstop.

"Yes...how nice," Charlotte said, braving the sea of Ramona's monologue.

"It's brilliant, you know."

"What is?"

"Lish's new book, of course."

"Of course. Yes, I'm sure it is."

"So we were wondering. No, I can't include Lish in this. We haven't discussed it, so I can't say for sure if it's on her mind. Anyhow, you know Lish, she'd never...But it stands to reason, doesn't it?"

"I beg your pardon? What stands to reason?"
"Well, we're both hoping that you'll review her book!"
"Ramona!" I cried, too late.
Peter, greeting Charlotte cordially, came to the rescue. "Let me introduce you to Sylvia Maxwell," he said.
Another agonized cry from me. "Oh, Peter!"
"But I'd love to meet her," Charlotte said, both of us following Peter to where Sylvia Maxwell stood. Until now Charlotte had been vaguely the special guest of honor. But she was easily and immediately displaced by La Maxwell. Bosom thrust forward like the prow of a ship, Sylvia reigned like a former great beauty, ignoring the fact that she had never been a beauty at all. It had to be obvious to Charlotte that in our circles Sylvia Maxwell was considered a grande personnage, not only by herself but by those around her, a fact underscored by the hush which attended her first remark.
"I'm sorry not to have read your version of Thackeray's great work," she informed Charlotte with a cold smile. "But I'm afraid I'm not overly acquainted with best sellers."
"Why should you be?" Charlotte said, and laughed. "In any case I never hoped to emulate that masterpiece. I merely took liberties with the title. Sin enough, I suppose."
"Resulting in great commercial success, however," Sylvia reminded Charlotte, unwilling to stop chewing this particular bone.
"I can't deny that," Charlotte said. The great lady nodded with satisfaction. "—but what is commercial success compared to great artistic achievement?"
Sylvia squinted, as if to determine whether Charlotte was pulling her leg, and decided she wasn't. "Perhaps we can continue this discussion another time," she said, and nodded to golden Peter, who smiled for all he was worth.
"I hope we do."
Peter took Sylvia's arm, preparatory to escorting her to her apartment in the building next door. She accepted this as homage due

her, but the joke was that Peter truly liked her, liked attending to her. She stopped to offer me the coolest of felicitations, and then she was gone.

A few sips of champagne, a few comments exchanged with what were clearly junior members of Peter's department, and it was time for Charlotte to go too. She had done her duty. I followed her into the bedroom to find her coat.

"I hate surprise parties," I said.

"Me too," Charlotte sympathized.

"I'm awfully sorry you were forced into this one."

"Forced into what? I enjoyed it."

"Well, I guess they meant well. Peter and Joey have been in collusion for weeks. And then Peter took me out to dinner tonight, and Joey wouldn't come and I pretended I didn't know why, and when I got home there was Joey, beaming away, and Ritz crackers were everywhere, and everyone—" I paused. "How did you find out about this by the way?"

Charlotte laughed. "Peter and I were in collusion too."

A funny moment. But the moment quickly resolved itself.

"Anyway, I'm particularly sorry you had to fall into Sylvia Maxwell's clutches."

"But sweetie, I really did want to meet her. You and Peter are probably too young to remember the Maxwells at their peak, but Edward Maxwell was absolutely it in those days. His essays, his lectures. Darling, they were fascinating. He put forgotten writers back on the map. And took contemporary fiction seriously, too. Which was practically unheard of, I assure you, in those days, when novelists had to be dead before they were even assigned in class, much less become subjects of a dissertation."

"A point of view I'm sure Sylvia still holds," I said, not disagreeing with her about Edward, only Sylvia. "Even though she's never stopped taking a free ride on Edward's coat tails. You must have seen some of her absurdly pretentious essays in Partisan Review et al, which I'm sure they only publish because she's the relict."

Charlotte smiled. "Well, Peter seems devoted to her."

"That's his ladies in distress syndrome."

I sank down onto the bed. "Which brings us back to Ramona. Oh, my god, I have to apologize for Ramona too. Believe me, Charlotte, I had no idea she was going to suggest that... In fact, I'm horrified that she even—"

"Sweetie, I don't write reviews, but I'd love to read your book," Charlotte said.

"Reunion? Really? Would you? Actually, I have an extra copy of the manuscript right here."

It was a sign of my new self-confidence. I once would have hemmed and hawed before giving Charlotte the manuscript, practically apologized for living. Ironic that Charlotte had given me the courage to impose on her.

"Great," she said. "I'll take it with me."

"But will you let me see your new book too?"

We sounded as if we were playing doctor.

"One of these days," Charlotte said. "Meanwhile, Lish, I'm afraid you're sitting on my coat."

"Oh, my god!"

I jumped up, thrust the manuscript which I had put into a Zabar's shopping bag, and her coat into her arms, and led her back into the living room. Peter had returned, and Joey had materialized too. The three of us stood in the doorway, saying goodbye, I ensconced between Joey on one side, Peter on the other, and my tacky living room as a backdrop.

"You're lucky," Charlotte said before she left.

Ironically, I assumed.

Now that everyone else had gone, Peter watched as I began to throw the dregs of my birthday party into the garbage can. (The last to leave was Ramona, naturally.) Blobby Ritz crackers, plastic champagne glasses whose stems had come off, crumpled napkins, empty bottles, leftover birthday cake stuck to paper plates, it all went in there.

"Un peu d'histoire," I said to Peter, who laughed at this private joke, a phrase lifted from one of the guidebooks we had assiduously studied on our honeymoon in France. First they would give a description of some point of interest, and then a bit of its history. But a perfect phrase for me too, at this moment, a woman with a distinct sense of being at a crossroads in her life. Leaving the garbage outside the kitchen door for pickup later, I wandered back into the diningroom where my cache of presents was heaped on the sideboard, next to my typewriter and a very small pile of new manuscript hastily covered with a blue silk scarf. It was true, what I had said to Charlotte, that gift soaps predominated. The bottle of Chivas Regal looked odd among them, though it would have under any circumstances. A strange present, really, but what had I expected from her? Earlier, Peter had given me a small gold circle pin, and Joey a little leatherette notebook for recording my loftier thoughts. I remembered their expectant smiles when they gave them to me, their excitement when I opened the door and everyone, Joey in the forefront, shouted "Surprise!" And felt like a rat for not being more grateful. Joey too had now appeared.

"I don't want to leave you with a mess, Ma," Joey said, whom like Peter, I had oversensitized to garbage.

"No, it's okay, you've both done enough."

"Really?" Peter said with a very intimate little lift of his eyebrow.

"Positive."

His disappointment registered. But it was one of those rare times when a party hadn't made me sexy. I shooed them off to bed, thanking them again and again, then flopped down in a chair in the living room to resume my contemplation of my life. I told myself it would help me decide what to put on my book jacket, though it was really to fend off a deepening depression.

"The author was born and brought up in Queens. Lousy childhood courtesy of virago mother and father perpetually hidden behind a newspaper. Best friend in high school Shirley Litvak, a math wiz who wore thick eyeglasses and shining silver braces. Author kept winning prizes in English, prompting mother to tell her no one would want to marry her if she was too smart. Come on from a lesbian in high sneakers in the gym locker room, prompting author to wonder if mother could be on the right track, was author queer in every sense of the word? Decides nobody fantasizing about heterosex so avidly day and night, could be homosex. Author enrolls at Barnard College where dating guys from Columbia settles the matter once and for all. Has discovered that in terms of boys, it's okay to be smart, but not to act it. (Would have told Shirley Litvak but somewhere en route SL has gotten engaged to a chiropractor.) Changes nickname from Allie to Lish.

"Immediately after graduation marries Peter Lasker, aka Ashley Wilkes, because she has now discovered it's also okay to get married to your dream man. Husband goes on to graduate work and an academic career at Columbia University. Author inaugurates own literary career as a secretary at the Ramona Brill Literary agency, where she imagines she will have time to pursue her own writing. She and husband are now equals, careerwise. 'Wait until you have a baby,' mother says grimly, father dying soon after, leaving mother unable to continue their quarrel with him, and author tearfully naming her son after him. Husband stops making the salad. Author quits agency and starts to write, piecework it's okay for a mother to do in the home, places a few short stories in such magazines as Steerage and Houndstooth, which pay off in free copies. Takes a deep breath and writes a novel, Classnotes of a Dreamer, which Ramona Brill miraculously manages to place with a small publisher. And now Reunion, which, despite early vicissitudes, is also scheduled for publication and already being considered by a major movie director for a minor motion picture…"

A success story, no? Poor Allie Morris, who I once was, would have given her eyeteeth to be in my present position. Shirley Litvak would have popped her braces. So what the hell was wrong with me tonight? Why was I so antsy and dispirited? It wasn't just birthday blues. Was this maybe a case of be careful what you wish for because you'll get it? No, because until tonight I'd been thrilled with what I'd gotten. I took a look around my living room seeing it again through Charlotte's eyes, as I had the minute she came in. It was all so incredibly tacky. Not only the Ritz crackers, and the champagne in plastic glasses whose stems kept falling off. And not only the furniture. No, it was the tenor of the whole evening. Ramona accosting Charlotte. Charlotte being condescended to by Sylvia Maxwell and being so nice about it. And then I, practically foisting my book on her. Sick with embarrassment, I finally went to bed, edging away from Peter's groping hand, and hoped for a dreamless sleep.

But in the morning Charlotte called to say she had stayed up all night reading my novel.

"Are you kidding?"

"No, really, I couldn't put it down. It's brilliantly handled. That metaphor of the college reunion—you pulled it off, Lish. I predict a great success with this one. You've become a terrifically assured writer. You've arrived."

"I have? I am? You do?"

She did. I was on cloud nine. Higher than when I'd first heard from Crutchworth. Higher than when Karl Brach started to make promising noises. At that moment it didn't even matter if I believed what Charlotte said, which I didn't. Yet. The point was that Charlotte believed it. Never mind the Chivas Regal and all the rest of it. She had just given me the birthday present I had been looking for maybe all my life. To have my best friend, the woman I had so long admired and now loved, tell me my book was wonderful, that I'd arrived.

6

The air on the Upper West Side was strangely warm and lazy for November. Indian summer, if you wanted to be poetic about it, not easy in my neighborhood. Still, there was a feeling of time out. Everything on hold. No important literary news on any of my fronts—Ramona, Crutchworth, Brach—which for the present was okay with me. No news was good news, or at least it wasn't bad news. No calls from Charlotte, either lately, which I put down to the general torpor. I had just come home from the supermarket, up to my chin with packages, having as usual gone out for only one thing and returned weighed down with many. Maybe after I put the groceries away I should poke around again at my third novel, which was still untitled and showing only small signs of life? But it was hard to launch a new project when the bets weren't in yet on the last one, no matter how reassuring Charlotte had been.

I yawned. A nap then? Like me, the apartment itself was mildly stuporous, the air so warm and almost tropical, there ought to have been a ceiling fan circling lazily overhead. I had just decided definitely on a nap before any major undertakings when the doorbell suddenly rang. I opened up, and there stood a messenger with a package addressed to Peter. I signed for it and then took what was obviously a manuscript into Peter's study and stuck it on his desk. Then, on impulse, I called Peter at his campus office to ask if maybe he'd like to have lunch. It had been a long time since we'd done that. In pre-Joey days, we'd steal back home afterward and make love. Love in the afternoon. It was different from other times. Sweeter, tenderer. Sexier too. But the English Department secretary told me he was out.

VANITY FARE

He seemed to be out a good deal, lately. Thoughts of a possible graduate student flickered through my mind and out again. No, idleness was just making me look for trouble.

I wondered what kind of manuscript had just arrived, anyway. Most stuff came to Peter's office, where he weeded it out before bringing what he needed to back home. Rarely did anything come directly here, certainly not by special messenger. Besides, this had a very professional look to it, and in fact was from Colophon Press, a decidedly commercial publisher. Come to think of it, Charlotte's new publisher. I wondered what else was on their list, and undid the wrappings, knowing Peter wouldn't mind. There was the usual gray cardboard manuscript box inside. Pasted on top was a label that read: Death on Venus, a novel by Charlotte Burns. Startling at first, then thrilling. The manuscript had obviously been meant for me, Mrs. Peter Lasker. (Charlotte had always been punctilious about such antiquated usages.) But never mind. Charlotte had sent me her book—she'd be horrified it had come to Peter instead—and I couldn't wait to read it. On a purely literary level, it was also extremely flattering. This was a long awaited work, after all, the first since Vanity Fare. Charlotte Burns and Alicia Morris, I thought. Perhaps one day, PhD candidates would do dissertations on how well we had known each other, how close we had been, maybe how we'd even gone to school together. (They probably wouldn't notice the age difference, which after a century or so wouldn't matter, anyway.) But when I opened the box there was a letter lying on top of the manuscript. And it wasn't addressed to Mrs. Peter Lasker. It was for Professor Peter Lasker.

"Dear Peter:
Charlotte told me you were eager to read this.
Wonderful. We look forward to hearing from you.
Cordially,
Arlene
Arlene Mott, Senior Editor

P.S. I'm hoping to persuade Charlotte to change the title
Maybe you can help? She's told me many time how much she
respects your judgement."

Surely there was some mistake. It was my opinion they wanted, a comment from me for the cover. Charlotte Burns was my friend. I was the feminist here. I was the one who had been waiting for this novel for years. Peter hadn't even heard of Vanity Fare until I told him about it. Knowing better, I read the damn letter again, and then over again. There was no mistake. It was Peter's opinion Arlene Mott was after. I remembered her all over him at Charlotte's dinner party and at the movie premiere. Oh, yes, this was all Arlene's doing. It had that bloodless bitch's stamp all over it. Probably, Charlotte knew nothing about this...And no, I wouldn't call her. If she hadn't already been told, she'd be terribly upset.

I left Peter's study and went into the living room where Vanity Fare sat in its place of honor on the bookshelves. I pulled it out, pausing at the inscription: "For Alicia Morris, all good wishes, Charlotte Burns." Had there really ever been a time when we knew each other so little? I thought of the two couples in the elevator glancing warily at each other, and shook my head, as at a baby picture. Charlotte's actual picture covered almost the entire back of the book jacket. Her head was thrown back, she was laughing. A corgi was in her lap, enjoying the joke. Since Charlotte hated dogs, who could have chewed up the furniture, and had resisted Cynthia's entreaties to get one, as she had once confessed to me, the animal was obviously a prop. The text said that Charlotte Burns had written a wicked satire. She lived in New York and the Hamptons with her husband and young daughter. I turned back to the first page, and settled down to read in one of our, oh so tacky, armchairs. Hours later, when early dusk was falling, I closed the novel. It was clever all right, highly professional. But strangely, it didn't impress me as it once had. Why had this book influenced us all so strongly years ago? Because it was a first strike in what turned out to be the women's movement, touching on so many quivering chords? I thought of what Cezanne had said of himself: "I am the primitive of the movement I started." Not that Charlotte Burns was Cezanne. She would laugh like hell at the idea.

It was Charlotte who called first. The next morning. Right on time. As soon as the husbands had left. I had said nothing about the manuscript to Peter, and he had said nothing to me. Possibly he hadn't noticed it in the pile on his desk. I thought of letting the phone ring, but I'd never had the spine to do that.

"Oh, sweetie," Charlotte said, launching into some story about making Basmati rice for dinner when in the middle of it one of Steven's loony patients called and the crust burned. Why was she suddenly making Basmati rice? Was she back in the world of Vanity Fare, which I had just come from? It was eerie.

Ordinarily I would have kidded her about it. But uncharacteristically, I was silent.

"Sweetie...? Is something wrong...?"

"Why should something be wrong?" I said.

"Uh, oh. Something is."

I assured her that everything was fine, that I'd call her later, that I'd suddenly developed a splitting headache... But Charlotte persisted. "Come on, sweetie. Tell me. Another love problem? I hope you're not knocked up."

I took a deep breath.

"Hey, I was kidding," she said.

"Charlotte," I began, trying to sound calm, "I don't want to upset you, but I have to tell you that your manuscript's in a box on Peter's desk. It was addressed to him. Colophon sent it over to our house yesterday."

"To your house?" Charlotte said. "Oh, god."

There was another silence from me, a long one. Until that moment I guess I really had believed it was all a silly mistake. Now I knew that the only mistake had been that the damned thing was supposed to go to Peter's office.

"It was Arlene's idea, sweetie," Charlotte said. "You know Arlene. We were having lunch at the Four Seasons and—"

"What the hell does the Four Seasons have to do with it?"

"It used to be so elegant," Charlotte said gaily. "Like a grand ocean liner. Now it's more like some showy cruise ship. Of course they still charge the earth for six grilled shrimp… And some of the old publishing types are still there…"

Long pause.

"She told me you wouldn't mind," Charlotte said.

"Really?"

"She said you'd understand that it was important that…She insisted."

"Important? She insisted? What is Colophon Press, a fascist dictatorship—?"

Charlotte started to laugh, even though she must have realized that I wasn't being funny.

"Why?" I said.

"It was the Maxwell Prize. Arlene thought—"

"The Maxwell Prize? My God, you can't be serious."

"Thank you."

The real joke, the terrible joke was that if she had sent it to me, I would have busted my butt to have Peter read the damn thing for whatever reason. Didn't she know that? How could Charlotte be such a fool, so callously ambitious? So willing to override everything we were to each other? Didn't she realize that in terms of collusion, of betrayal this was almost as bad as if she had slept with Peter? Maybe even worse, since one involved passion, the other calculation—though only Charlotte, god help me, could have understood that.

I hung up. She called back. I didn't answer.

She sent me a letter on embossed stationery. "Lish, darling, you're taking this all too seriously. I was eager for both your opinions..."

Like hell, she was.

"What difference does an address on a box make? This is a silly contretemps. I'm the best friend you've ever had."

I didn't answer that either.

Then she called to wish me a happy Thanksgiving, a holiday I had once said was my favorite. Nobody mentioned Peter.

"I wish you well too, Charlotte," I said.

"Come on, Lish, why the lofty tone? We're friends, for godssake"

Friends? There was a time I thought of us as sisters. "Thank you for calling."

"This is high school stuff," Charlotte said.

Then it turned gray and cold. Bleak and Christmas time. Then a bleaker January. One day, going down Fifth Avenue after seeing Ramona and also returning a sale item, I saw Charlotte and Arlene coming up the street toward me. Maybe on their way back from lunch at the Four Seasons, though I didn't know where that was. Both women were wrapped in their black minks. I wore a red coat that I suddenly realized was too long and absolutely the wrong color for me. Charlotte smiled. I nodded back. Next to her, Arlene's eyes were like black daggers. She put her hand protectively under Charlotte's elbow, as if she were Charlotte's fight handler. Nobody spoke, nobody slowed down. But it was a moment frozen in time that I knew would play itself out over and over again. Like that scene from Charlotte's movie.

"Why so glum?" Peter said when I got home. "Didn't Ramona ever manage to get to the point?"

"No."

But that wasn't news. Peter was looking to me for the rest of it.

"This new coat's all wrong. I'm too heavy and short for it. It makes me look like a windup toy. A Russian folk dancer."

"What brought this on?"

"I ran into her on Fifth Avenue."

"Oh, Christ," Peter said, "are we going to go all over that again?"

He was right. We'd already tossed this baby around many times and always ended up with Peter saying something amused and exasperated that ended with the word women. He really had nothing to do with it anyway. He pointed out that he had never been interested in Charlotte's work in the first place—I was the one who had foisted it on him—and he had certainly done nothing to further the new book's success. No quote. Nothing. Certainly no serious consideration for the Maxwell Prize, which was probably going to an eighty-year old male novelist who taught in Davenport, Iowa. Somewhere along the line Charlotte's title had been changed to Venus and Adonis, but that certainly didn't seem like the result of Peter's influence either, anymore than did the piles of the novel already in bookstores well in advance of the actual publication date.

Peter was smiling at me so engagingly, damn him, that I could hardly stay angry. He didn't understand. He had never understood the beginning of Charlotte and me—why should he understand the ending? I let the matter drop, and Peter patted me convivially on the shoulder, the way he did Joey. The phone rang, and when Peter came back from answering, he gave me the great news that Herb Lobel was giving another one of his parties. A new girlfriend had preoccupied him through the usual end of the year festivities and right through Valentine's Day. But Herb wasn't also going to let the Ides of March and the beginning of spring go by, no matter how cold the weather.

Of course Charlotte would be there. That went without saying. As we got into Herb's elevator, I remembered, as I always did, the two unacquainted couples glancing away from each other awkwardly. Peter and I put our coats on the pile of other coats in the small room with the king sized bed that constituted Herb's bedroom. Then we entered a somewhat larger low ceilinged space that was his living room. My apartment might be typical Upper West Side, but this was typical jerry-built East Side. Just the pad for someone like Herb. I stuck my arm firmly through Peter's and looked around at the usual guests being bored with each other.

Charlotte was there, all right, alone on the sofa where we had first started to chat, waiting, as if she expected me to come back and sit beside her. She was wearing a silky short black jersey dress, one arm draped along the sofa back, her red nail polish no doubt perfectly applied, her hair in an elegant chignon, her slender legs, in dark stockings, crossed at the knees. Ready to be photographed for a society page in Vogue. Nothing about her suggested that Venus and Adonis had finally been reviewed in the Sunday Times, weeks and weeks late, one of the worst, most scathing reviews I had ever read, written, amazingly, by her "good friend" Nancy Tarkov. What would this do to the piles of books in the stores waiting to be snapped up? I wondered if Charlotte and Arlene had already got wind of that review the day I ran into them on Fifth Avenue. If I had known about it too, would I have stopped to talk, to console? Charlotte had looked forlorn, as if Arlene were propping her up. Great. One sighting of Charlotte and already I was getting all entangled again emotionally. I turned toward Peter, wanting to go right back home. But Peter had detached himself from me and headed for the thick of things.

Trying to avoid Charlotte altogether, I made my way to the makeshift bar in Herb's dining room, right off his kitchenette. Herb's latest girlfriend wasn't in immediate evidence, but there was the clone of an old one hanging around, red haired this time instead of blond. Or was it the same one and she had dyed her hair? Whoever this was had some lower echelon job with New Directions, and was eager to sound literary. Incredibly, her subject was the fictional uses of ambiguity.

"I was thinking about that myself," I said.

"Life imitates art," she said, eager to discuss that too.

Herb was beaming. He had beamed the same way with his self-styled Cuban spitfire and the smiling Japanese, both of whom were also standing around. Herb had a habit of making friends out of discards.

"There is no ambiguity in exile!" the Cuban declared, her eyes flashing. "I feel myself always to be an exile!"

Herb beamed harder. The Cuban's claim to being literary was that she had once had an affair with a Spanish language writer. It became imperative to go find Peter. But at the doorway to the living room, I paused. Through a knot of people I could glimpse Charlotte still alone on the sofa, a mannequin in black.

"Ah, here you are, my swan," her husband Steve said to me, coming up to give me a kiss on the cheek.

I kissed him back. Why not? I nothing against him, after all. I stupidly thought of commiserating with him about Charlotte's awful review, and remembered it wasn't my business. We stood there for a moment smiling at each other, two people sending vaguely affectionate signals across a divide. Then he gave me a hug and drifted away.

Several guests were going past with paper plates full of Herb's usual deli fare, on the way back from the diningroom. Peter appeared on his way to get some too. I caught his arm urgently.

"Let's split, sweetheart," I said.

"We just got here," Peter told me.

"I know. But I suddenly don't feel well. Not well enough for Herb's salami, anyhow."

"You look okay. Maybe you could just have the potato salad."

"Peter, let's go home. Please?"

"Okay, in a minute," Peter said, turning to talk to our genial host Herb, who had begun to walk around urging everybody to eat something. I looked into the living room, and saw that Steve Aaronson had sat down on the sofa and was murmuring something to Charlotte. She nodded and got up. Thank God, they were leaving the party, Charlotte trailing behind her husband. So with a little luck I could avoid her altogether. But I was wrong. Charlotte made a detour straight over to where I was. She stopped in front of me.

"Steven and I are going out to dinner, Lish," she said. "A real dinner. Why don't you and Peter join us?"

"No, not tonight, thank you."

"Why not? Sweetie, you abominate these cold cuts as much as I do."

"Hi, Charlotte," Peter said, turning back. Charlotte gave a little, very unattractive and very uncharacteristic girlish moue. "What's the matter?"

"Lish doesn't want to have dinner with us."

"She doesn't feel well."

"She's fine," Charlotte said, cocking her head and smiling, as if the next step would be twisting his buttonhole. Why the hell couldn't she let it alone?

"I'd like to go home, Peter," I said.

He hesitated, looking from one to the other of us.

"Now."

I dragged him into the bedroom, retrieved our coats, shoved his at Peter, and propelled him out of the party. Steve Aaronson looked at us kind of sadly when we went by, but said nothing.

"You didn't have to behave like that," Peter said, as we stood in the cold looking for a taxi.

He finally hailed one and we climbed in.

"Behave like what?"

"You know what."

"Really?" I said, after he had shut the door. "And what about you when she was simpering and winding you around her little finger?"

"Simpering? Wow. She only wanted to go out to dinner. What's the big deal?"

"It's a big deal to me. You just prefer not to understand."

Peter sighed. "I think you prefer not to also."

"Really? Well, I'm out there in the real literary world. Depending on loyalty and yes, sisterhood. Not loftily bestowing laurel leaves on safe academic contenders."

"Come on, Lish. Forget the laurel leaves and sisterhood. You've always been jealous of Charlotte Burns and you know it. That's what this is really all about."

I paused, letting the partial truth of that sink in. "Well, maybe I was jealous once," I said, "but I can assure you this worm has turned."

"Make up your mind, Lish. You're either a worm or a contender," Peter told me.

I turned to him in a rage. God knew what next flew out of my mouth, or out of his, for that matter. It was the first really bad quarrel we'd ever had, and ended with Peter walking into his study and solidly closing the door.

I sat alone in the living room, hungry, furious, miserable. She had done it again, pissed on everything I cared about. My relationship with my husband, my inner peace, yes and my dinner too. I could still picture her using those ridiculously flirtatious wiles on Peter, those ridiculously outdated wiles, then ratting on me like a schoolgirl. "Lish won't have dinner with us…blah, blah, blah…" The woman was shameless. There was nothing she wouldn't stop at to get her way. Trying to grapple with her was like climbing a glass wall. There were no handholds. The more I thought about it, the more enraged I became. Then the goddamn doorbell rang.

It rang and rang and rang. Joey said he'd get it.

Then, incredibly, I heard Charlotte Burns' voice demand, "Where's your mother?"

Without waiting for an answer, she stormed into the living room where I was sitting on the couch, her Blackgama mink coat open and slapping at her legs. I stared. What chuzpah! What the hell did she think she was doing here?

"What are you doing here, Charlotte?" I said.

"Lovely welcome. Thank you, sweetie. You know why I'm here."

"Actually, I don't." I stood up, indicating that she should leave, but she planted herself down where I had been sitting, clearly determined not to budge until she had everything straightened out. To her satisfaction, of course.

"Oh, Lish," she demanded, "what was so terrible about what I did? Why are you being so cruel? This isn't like you."

"Listen, Charlotte, it's late. Please, just go home, okay?" I said, not knowing what else to do. "We'll talk about it another time."

"I'm not leaving until you understand. Why are you doing this to us? Sweetie, you're nuts to do this to us. I never betrayed you. It was Arlene."

"Okay, so it was Arlene."

"I loved you. I thought of you as my—"

Thought of me as her what? She paused, as if she were trying hard to think, trying to remember. I wondered suddenly it she were drunk.

"I really was your best friend," she tried again. "Am your best friend. I saw in you what nobody else did. The promise....then Arlene forced me to…"

"Where's Steve?" I said.

"Steve? Steven? I don't know…"

She probably didn't. She looked around and caught sight of herself in the mirror that hung opposite the sofa. That old fiction writer's trick. If so, then maybe she realized she looked like Leah at the end of Cheri. Haggard, acting like a lunatic. But Colette had brought us together.

"Oh, sweetie!" Charlotte said, as if she had thought of this too, rising and embracing me.

I tried to undo her, but she clung tighter. She was drunk, all right. I smelled booze. Over her head, I saw Joey watching us from the entrance to the living room. I had forgotten him. How could I have forgotten him? Then there was Peter, who had suddenly appeared too. Peter looked at me coldly.

"It's okay, Charlotte," I said, avoiding that look. "Calm down. It's all right. Everything's going to be all right."

"No, you don't understand! It won't be! It can't be! You mustn't hate me. I love you. We have to talk. We have to—"
She was crying now, but I had succeeded in unlocking her arms.
"Peter will get you a cab," I said.
Silently, Peter came in and took her by the hand. She stopped crying and walked out with him, like a surrendered prisoner. Now Peter was looking no longer cold. But very sad. And very sweet.

Joey had stayed back in the doorway, a young, skinny, and very troubled boy.
"Why don't you and Charlotte get together and beat the crowd?" Joey said, with a fake sophisticated laugh.
"Shut up, Joey," I said, wearily. "You don't know what the hell you're talking about." And thanked Charlotte Burns for yet another mess she had made in my life.
Still, out of the mouths of babes? I could still feel Charlotte's clinging arms. The hennaed hair rubbing against my neck, her coat engulfing us in mink. The liquor fumes. The liquor explained a lot. Why she had come where she wouldn't be welcome? How she could have so abandoned any pretense of dignity?
Peter returned from getting her a taxi, but said nothing. Then we both went to bed and lay in the darkness, thinking side by side.

A series of jagged, confused dreams woke me at about three in the morning, "the dark night of the soul," as Scott Fitzgerald had put it, the hour when people gave in to despair. I thought of reading, but knew that would do no good. I slipped out of bed anyhow and on the dining room mantel, near my portable typewriter, was the bottle of Chivas Regal Charlotte had given me for my birthday, still untouched. I took it into the living room, opened it for the first time, and poured out a generous drink. Not my kind of thing, which had never gone beyond gingerly experimentation with pot, though I was beginning to guess it was very much Charlotte's. A secret drinker in addition to everything else? Tonight's snootful had probably been no exceptional event. How come I never even knew that? Ma semblable, ma soeur. Ha! Well, maybe I could at least find out what Charlotte felt like when she was drinking this stuff.

Making myself comfortable on the couch, I knocked back the stiff slug of the Scotch. I knew it was supposed to be aged and mellow, besides being expensive, but it burned and tasted medicinal. Undaunted, I tried another, then another, and then lost count. Soon there was no more burning, just a nice warm glow in the region of my heart. It was still night outside... My eyes closed... I was floating in the sky, floating, contentedly floating. I looked down, and there was a football field. Little anxious people were scurrying around on it, like agitated mice. How foolish they were. Couldn't they see it was all just a game? A game without any meaning? But you could rise above it if you wanted to. Yes, a lovely, seductive voice at my shoulder was telling me so. Forget that silly frenzy. Leave it all below. Float up here in peace, serenity, bliss...

"Wake up," Peter said.

"No, leave me alone. I'm not finished."

"Wake up, Lish."

I opened my eyes reluctantly. It wasn't easy. They hurt. I was still in the living room and sharp daylight was everywhere.

Peter was giving me a funny look. "Charlotte's dead."

"What? Ah, so that's who it was."

I nodded and closed my eyes again, settling back into my dream. Yes, of course it was Charlotte's voice at my shoulder. I should have known. So wonderfully seductive.

"It's okay," I murmured. "She's happy now. Life's only a game."

"For Chrissakes, snap out of it!" Peter said. "Charlotte's dead. She threw herself out of the window last night!"

7

Naturally, the funeral was at a very good address, Campbell's on Madison Avenue, a discreet and decidedly nondenominational establishment, preferred host for many celebrity interments. From the entrance it could have been a small expensive European hotel—like Charlotte, totally comme il faut. But of course it was impossible to imagine her being buried from a place like Riverside Memorial Chapel, over on the West Side, with everybody carrying on. I had come prepared to carry on myself, but it was impossible even to cry in that atmosphere. I could only too clearly hear Charlotte say, with that little moue of hers, "Oh, sweetie, come on." Even Peter seemed totally uncomfortable, drawing away when I tried to squeeze his hand. It wasn't his ambience. It wasn't anybody's. We all sat there glued and frozen, stuck, waiting to get out, have a drink, talk about how long we had known Charlotte, how we had never expected, etc. And, ultimately, what had made her do it? An old Gorham classmate, whom I had never heard of or laid eyes on before had spoken of "Charlie," and who the hell was that? Then Mort Glasgow, her first editor, offered a little critique of Charlotte's contributions to literature, discreetly downplaying the fact that in its day Vanity Fare had also been a terrific money maker. Then Karl Brach, who had made Vanity Fare into a movie and with whom it now occurred to me she had probably had an affair. (As with Sam Cuccio, who was notably absent?) Nothing from Arlene Mott, not surprising, since her forte had always been fraught silences.

Now, to my dismay, Charlotte's daughter Cynthia mounted the platform behind the coffin, holding a wavering piece of paper. I thought of my Joey, safely at home. Goddamn it, whose idea was it to have this wan and tremulous creature, whose pale hair girlishly floated down behind her back like Alice in Wonderland's, make a public speech, and about a mother who had just recently thrown herself from a fifteen-story window on Park Avenue? Did Steve, the psychiatrist, think it would have some therapeutic value? In which case, why had Steve himself lied in the obit and listed the cause of death as a "short illness"? Very short, maybe thirty seconds worth. But there we all were: fellow writers, major and minor New York literati, academics, shrinks, hangers-on—sitting there like an audience, not one of us knowing what to do when real death, not metaphor struck. I was foolishly sore at Charlotte for putting us through this, neatly enclosed in her coffin, though God knew in what messed up and shattered physical state, that woman so fastidious her red fingernail polish never suffered a chip, and who had once laughingly confessed to me that when the maid was gone, she went after the corners of her apartment with Q-tips. But that was the point. It had all been so funny and bright in the beginning, a sophisticated game. Except that Charlotte, who seemed to know the rules better than anyone, had broken them all. And herself into the bargain.

I needn't have worried about her daughter, though. Cynthia was more unruffled than I had ever seen her. She compared her mother's life to Schubert's Unfinished Symphony, though I didn't recall Charlotte being musically inclined. Maybe again, this was Steve's influence. We all sighed when she had finished, wiping our eyes, which were dry. Then the rabbi said Kaddish, introducing a startlingly Jewish note into the proceedings. I kept forgetting Charlotte was Jewish. But it was a carefully intoned and articulated Kaddish, nothing like the one at my father's funeral, which had reduced my mother and the older relatives to hysterics. We finally and decorously filed out, leaving Charlotte behind, like the hostess at a party. I looked back at the coffin. Goodbye, Charlotte, I thought, though I can't believe you're really in there.

VANITY FARE

I was holding Peter's hand firmly now, as we all assembled haphazardly on the sidewalk. The hearse was waiting and so were the limousines that were to carry Steve and Cynthia and other bereaved near and dear to the cemetery. Later on, some of us at Steve's invitation, had been asked to regather at the Aaronson apartment. But we couldn't disperse yet. We didn't know what to do with ourselves. It was still like a party, except outdoors in a cold sunshine, and any chitchat now was pointless. We hung around, anyway, bulky and awkward in our overcoats. I was longing to get rid of mine—the too-long, red one—permanently. A few of Charlotte's more distant connections nodded coolly in my direction. No call for conversation there, either. We had been introduced by somebody, but I couldn't remember whether by my own name, my writing name or by my married name, though it was supremely idiotic to worry about it now. There was also a motley group unknown to any of us, fetched possibly by the obituaries. The crowd was starting to disperse. I heard someone begin yet another tired Gerald Ford joke—we had already rehashed Watergate ad nauseum—and when I realized that Peter was about to start the usual discussion with Herb Lobel about their joint seminar on Victorian sexuality at Columbia, I pulled him away by the hand. I wanted to be alone with my husband, to let silly, irrelevant quarrels be part of the past, to be solaced by him, reassured that my life was okay and in good shape.

We went across the street to the East Side Pub, which was small and dark, well suited to the occasion. We'd gone there after other funerals at Campbell's but always when it was a minor acquaintance, not someone we had known well. Peter still had on his somber funeral face, an expression at odds with his innocently boyish air, his bright blue eyes, his blond handsomeness. More than ever today I had trouble believing this guy was my husband. Still my own Ashley Wilkes. Jewish, yes, but WASP Jewish, like Charlotte. A man I could always make smile.

But Peter wasn't smiling now. We had ordered white wine and tuna fish sandwiches. He was quietly drinking his wine and I was starting on the second half of my sandwich.

"Oh, God," I said, putting it down with disgust. How could I be eating at a time like this? I can't believe—"

"Don't talk about it, Lish," Peter said.

"Okay, sweetheart."

He looked so distressed that I, who had wanted to be consoled, now wanted only to console him. But Peter was right. The subject was best entirely avoided. He ordered two more glasses of wine and I looked at my watch in the semi-gloom. There was still lots of time before the gathering at the Aaronsons, which I was more and more dreading, and what were we supposed to do meanwhile? Treat this like an ordinary day, which it wasn't? Go all the way home to Claremont Avenue, then back to the East Side again? Not enough time. Take a walk? I was in heels. A movie would have been great, my usual solution to everything, but it would take too long and was hardly appropriate under the circumstances. Maybe Peter would have an answer. But Peter never hung himself up on such dilemmas. I reached out my hand to him anyway. I wanted to ask him why I felt so numb, why I couldn't cry, why in spite of myself I had finished the whole tuna fish sandwich. But he abruptly pushed my hand aside and threw some money down on the table.

"You killed her," Peter said quietly, getting up.

"I what?"

He shook his head. "I'll meet up with you later."

"Peter! What did you say? What are you talking about?"

But he had already picked up his coat from the hook near the bar and started out the door. I stared after him, flabbergasted. "Peter!"

One of us was crazy. The door closed. I was alone in that dark funereal place. I couldn't believe it. Peter had never done anything like this before. It was totally out of character. And what was he talking about? Killed her? Surely I had misheard him. Maybe he'd just wanted me to stop going on about Charlotte. Or about tuna fish. Would he reappear at the Aaronsons? Was that what he'd meant by catching up with me later? I was totally at sea. Now I really began to cry. For every reason in the world. I wept buckets. I finally pulled myself together, murmuring cravenly as I put Peter's money down at the cash register, "Funeral." But what was I to do now? I still couldn't go home, even by taxi. I was afraid that Peter wouldn't be there when I arrived. Or that he would, and then what would he say? I started to walk down Madison Avenue, still teary at first. Then I gradually calmed down enough to glance into a few boutique windows. Only glance. This was Charlotte's turf, not mine. Charlotte, with her reedy figure and unmistakable air of money. Charlotte, who had to be talked into that wildly expensive mink coat by Steve and then treated it as if it were worthless. I had never begrudged her the money—well, maybe a little—but mostly the figure. (I doubted that she had ever truly realized we weren't in the same financial league.) She had been wearing the mink the night she barged in on me, the night she died. I wondered if she was wearing it when she threw herself out the window

In spite of myself I looked east and there was Charlotte's apartment building in the distance. She had lived very high up. I shook my head and quickly walked over to Fifth Avenue, where I took the first bus downtown. There was still plenty of time before I had to come uptown again for the Aaronson's funeral gathering, at which I had to appear. (But, of course Peter would be there too, wouldn't he?) When I finally realized that the bus had already passed the Forty-second Street Library, my original destination, I got off at Lord and Taylor. Compared to my mood the perfumed atmosphere in the store was unhingingly cheerful. Though it was winter outside, here there were signs of summer everywhere. White jewelry, straw hats, organza scarves, which made cold weather unreal. At the Elizabeth Arden cosmetics counter I impulsively sat down for one of the free makeups they were offering. I knew I was a fright, that the crying had wreaked havoc with my mascara, left raccoon circles around my eyes, sooty streaks down my cheeks. However, the cosmetics lady seemed unfazed. I closed my eyes as she patted, prattled, wiped, applied cremes, astringents, concealers, lip rouge. Maybe when she was finished I really would be made over, become gorgeous, fearless. But after about fifteen minutes when she held up the mirror—that old mirror trick again—what I looked like was embalmed. And on top of that, she had given me thick black eyebrows like Bette Davis in Whatever Happened to Baby Jane? Great. It was the perfect look for the gathering at the Aaronsons, which though I continued to try to think of it as a party, was obviously going to be a wake.

When I walked in, having been so worried about arriving early, I was late. Many of the group who had also been at the funeral were already leaving. Steve was stationed just inside the living room, saying goodbye—poor guy, it was his day for saying goodbye. He was holding hands with Cynthia, who was awkwardly receiving hushed compliments on her eulogy. Steve gave me a big hug and a kiss, and told me he was glad I had come. He meant it. I took back the mean things I had thought about him at Campbell's. He seemed to be a very decent guy, really, reliable, safe as houses, though I felt stupidly disloyal to Charlotte for even having such ideas pass through my mind.
"We were wondering where you were," Steve said.
"We?"
Surely he didn't mean Cynthia, who had let go of his hand and wandered away. No, he meant Peter, who had come up behind him, smiling his boyish smile. I couldn't believe my eyes. Not that Peter was there, but that he looked as if nothing had happened in the bar, that he hadn't said anything. Maybe he hadn't and the pressure of Charlotte's suicide had driven me mad.
"I was at Lord and Taylor to kill time," I explained stupidly to them both, wondering too late how I had managed to stumble across that particular phrase.

But Steve only laughed and turned to the next departing guest.

"I wasn't shopping," I said to Peter. "I was having a makeup done because I was crying. But now I think I look embalmed." Another unfortunate metaphor.

"You look great," Peter said, ignoring it.

I examined his face far more carefully than he had examined mine. But there was no trace of anything amiss. He was his old relaxed and easy-going self. He turned back to Steve. Behind them the living room was steadily emptying out, but I felt that because I had come so late I should stay a while longer. Usually at such a pause in a gathering, the choice would be either to wander off toward the bookshelves, or look out the window. Unfortunately, Arlene Mott was standing by the bookshelves. "It's a crumbling world," she was saying to nobody I knew. "People are easily discarded, easily forgotten." She caught my eye, or I caught hers. Whichever came first, didn't matter. I fled over to the big windows, draped in long ivory silk, and automatically and fearfully looked out.

But the Park Avenue view was totally unthreatening. It was a street that could buy its seasons. The crowds of russet mums that had been there in the autumn had been wrenched from their beds, replaced by elegant spindly white Christmas trees whose lights twinkled for block after block. Then Christmas too had been wrested away, and now in something of a seasonal hiatus, shiny expensive greenery filled the beds and would stay there until spring, when suddenly the traffic islands swayed with masses of bright red and yellow tulips. I looked away. Thoughts of spring brought back other springs.

At a nearby window sill, Cynthia was busily watering some exotic plants, that clearly didn't need watering. She evidently thought of herself as some kind of au pair. In the Hamptons, she had needed to be torn away from the kitchen. But Steve clearly wasn't buying any of it. He came up and whispered to her, gently taking the watering can from her hand. She nodded and went off to her bedroom a little way down the hall. In the few moments the door was open, I glimpsed lots of dotted Swiss, a pink vanity table, a small flowered settee. The dream room of a teen aged girl, or the dream of the mother of a teen aged girl—who was never to grow up.

Now the living room was almost empty of guests, but filled with Charlotte. Her delicate antique furniture, the elegant and slender gilded tables, those long ivory draperies, the occasional silk paisley throw. Beautiful, tasteful, silent, and waiting, like the furniture in a museum room. A red velvet rope in the doorway wouldn't have been a surprise. I wondered who would take care of it now? Who would follow after the maid, cleaning the corners with Q-tips? I looked around at Peter, who was still smiling cheerfully and had even come and put his arm around my shoulder. I flinched, remembering the pub. Then I told myself that even Peter was entitled to lose his cool sometimes. But had he really said what I imagined I'd heard, that I'd driven Charlotte to suicide? Unthinkable thought, which I knew would come up to haunt me later. Haunt me? Never mind. Right now all I wanted to do was go home, and the bottom line was that Peter would take me home. Still, how strange…that there should ever have come a time when I would be so eager to leave Charlotte's beautiful apartment.

8

News of Charlotte's death, though not her suicide, was soon circulating all over the place, in the tabloids, even on the radio. The Times obit, good sized, included the laughing picture from the back flap of Vanity Fare, which was dated 1963. Colophon Press ran a black bordered memorial notice, which was more advertising than they had done for Venus and Adonis. Maybe one day I would read the damn thing, but not yet. Especially since I understood there was a graphic scene in it about a deranged woman throwing herself out the window. Naturally, in her nasty review, Nancy Tarkov had found that part unconvincing.

By now, everyone had stories about Charlotte's suicide, different takes on how it had actually happened. That poor Cynthia was in the room when Charlotte jumped. That she wasn't. That Steve was in the room, grabbing for Charlotte, that he wasn't. That Cynthia was out and had come home to find her mother splattered down below, cops looking down too. That she had fainted and when revived given the police her father's phone number, and he refused to come at first.

For myself, I kept wondering stupidly how long the fall had lasted, and if Charlotte had suddenly realized what she was doing and horribly changed her mind in the middle. I wondered if she cared what a bloody mess she was going to make of her slender, carefully groomed body, her perfect fingernails. Other nutty things kept going round and round in my head. I thought of calling Steve and saying, "It's okay, she's happy now"—but even I understood that wouldn't do. I did tell Herb's latest girlfriend at some point that life was a football field, but this one was a potter and luckily she never quite grasped anything anyone was saying. And sometimes still my hand would reach for the telephone before it remembered and made a fist. There was a time—could it be only a little over a year ago?—when I would have babbled to Peter about this strange, recurring angst. But Peter had accused me of killing Charlotte, and no matter how convincingly he denied it, and even if I had imagined it, I couldn't connect with him in the old way anymore—not even in bed. Herb Lobel had once mentioned in another connection that distrust diminished sexual desire. So maybe this also happened when you flew too close to the sun. Or what you thought was the sun.

"She came here," I said to Joey. "She was in this room. I could have stopped her, don't you see? She was reaching out to me."

Maybe this was what Peter had meant?

"Oh, come on, Ma," Joey said. "Everybody who knew her is probably feeling that way."

But Joey looked worried. Really worried about me. I smiled at him to reassure him that I was okay, though I wasn't. I was sick.

Herb Lobel had reluctantly agreed to meet me and talk. The café outside the Hotel Stanhope was his idea. Posh enough to be impersonal, it was also convenient to his office. An elegant upper Fifth Avenue scene stretched out on all sides, including a splendid view of the Metropolitan Museum of Art across the street. Weatherwise, the April afternoon was perfection. In fact, Herb Lobel and I might have been idle tourists, except that Herbie looked pinched and edgy, as if I had caught him between analytic sessions, which no doubt I had.

"I've come up with several names for you, Lish," Herb said finally, after we had chatted about the lovely weather, that Karl Brach had optioned my book, and that the Vietnam War had at last petered out to a dismal, official end.

I looked at the slip of paper he was handing me. It had been torn from a prescription pad.

"I don't know, Herbie," I said. "Maybe this wasn't such a hot idea, after all. Maybe working for the ERA, or something, would be more positive, more sustaining. What do you think?"

"Come on, Lish, we all need help once in a while."

"We do?"

"Certainly. By the way—delicate question—have you ever gone to anyone before?"

"A couple of times. When I was in college."

"Really? You never mentioned it."

"It was before I met you and Peter. He made me nervous. The shrink, not Peter. He kept saying, 'It takes two to tango.'"

"Yes," Herb said. "Well, sometimes a small phrase—"

"Also he had this terrible cough. Which he said he and his own analyst were working on and tracing back, until one day it was finally diagnosed—by a real doctor, he admitted—as whooping cough. He'd picked it up in one of the children's wards he was working in. Can you imagine?"

"Yes," Herb said again, this time with a deep sigh. "...Well, if these names don't work out I can always come up with some more. Incidentally, you didn't say whether you preferred a man or a woman, so I put down both."

"A man! I want a man!" I blurted out.

"It's okay, Lish," Herb said gently. "There are men on that list too."

He didn't understand. Actually, neither did I.

Though the reason for our meeting was technically over, Herb and I continued to sit there, I slowly sipping at my gin and tonic, he at his white wine and soda. It occurred to me that, like Steve, though the context was different, Herb was actually a very nice guy. More attractive too than I usually gave him credit for. A bit too skinny and simian perhaps, but always with a very pleasant expression on his face. I could see what the bimbos, as Charlotte had called them, saw in him. (Though never what he saw in the bimbos.) He would make an admirable husband. Unfailingly kind, openly affectionate. A man who could read your heart and not be judgmental. Sitting there with him was almost like being on a date, he had made it all so relaxed and pleasant instead of clinical (aside from the prescription blank) so good-natured and truly interested. I had a sudden early memory, of me and Herb going to a party together one time when Peter was busy with his dissertation. It was a beautiful night but afterwards Herb was driving me back home the shortest and ugliest way. "Oh, Herb, do we have to?" I said, referring to the route, and he'd said, "Honey, I can't tonight." At the time it had given me a disturbingly vivid idea of his private life. Though he did laugh when it all got straightened out. Had this memory surfaced as just another example of his amiability or did it have some deeper significance? Herb was experiencing something similar, I could tell. Our smiles had assumed more meaning. It really did take two to tango.

Whatever the spell was that we had been under, Herb snapped out of it. He cast about for the waiter and the check, and glanced importantly at his watch, once more every inch a psychiatrist.

"Look, Lish, I've got to get back now. Let me know if there's anything more I can do for you. If those names don't work out—"

He sounded as he had the night he mistakenly thought I wanted him to take me home and screw me. There was the same embarrassed air of apology.

"Actually, there is something," I interrupted, before he could make good his getaway. "Herb, what's your take on Charlotte's suicide? Why do you think she killed herself?"

The super friendly smile vanished.

"I can't discuss that, Lish."

"Why not? We're friends. It's not as if you were her psychiatrist."

Silence, as Herb reached for the check and took care of it. He couldn't have been her psychiatrist. She'd made fun of him all the time, said she could even hear him smile over the phone.

"I mean, why? She had everything. She was at the top of the world."

"Nobody has everything," Herb said. I knew he was going to say that. So why was I sore that he did?

I must have seemed a shade desperate myself. Herb laughed his pointless laugh. I guess he figured one female novelist of his acquaintance off the deep end was enough.

"Look, honey, I really do have to leave now," Herb said. "I'd offer you a lift, but my office is just around the corner."

"It's okay, Herbie. I want to stick around here for a while anyway."

"Well, let me know what happens. If these won't do, I'll find you some more." He hesitated. "And best to Peter."

"Best to—" I almost said, "—to the latest..." I could never remember any of their names, except what I called them in my head. "The Potter...Chiquita Banana...The Dead Mouse..."

Without waiting for me to end my hesitation, Herb gave me a quick kiss on the cheek and departed. I ordered another gin and tonic to pay for on my own, though it cost the earth, and sipped it slowly. It tasted like summer. But summer brought back that weekend in East Hampton, and Charlotte relentlessly swimming back and forth in her pool, and never fished out. Would I see her that way for the whole rest of my life? I took Herb's list of psychiatrists and stuck it in my wallet alongside a credit slip from Bloomingdale's. Maybe another time. Anyway, poor Herb probably needed a shrink as much as I did at the moment, maybe more. Judging from his reticence, though not Charlotte's doctor, he was still a psychiatrist. If I imagined I'd somehow failed to prevent her suicide, what must Herb think? Steve also, come to think of it. What, in fact, had psychiatry in general done for Charlotte? And what might it do to me? Roil my mind irreparably, lead to shock treatment, send me flying out a window also? No, I knew I'd never have the nerve to jump. Sleeping pills were more my style. The big dreamer, the last big dream. Pills and booze. Though why was I thinking of dying on this lovely spring day? I wasn't really even unhappy. Just, from time to time—sick.

I finished my drink and paid the check, but still didn't want to go home. I called from the corner and left the usual message with Joey about frozen chicken pot pies, including one for Melissa if necessary—would my life never get beyond those damn pies?—then took a cab over to a small First Avenue theater where "Vanity Fare" had been revived because of the interest aroused by Charlotte's newsworthy death. It was still pretty early, so the audience was sparse. Just me and a few scattered elderly people in the dark. Their presence made me uneasy, and brought back thoughts of death again. What must it be like to have so much time and yet so little? I made myself focus on the screen. After many previews of attractions yet to come, the movie—film?—started. Credits began rolling across the screen. Karl Brach's name was everywhere, and so was the name of everybody else who had contributed to the production. Except Charlotte's. I began to panic. Where was Charlotte? Was she no longer even here? I finally saw "Based on the novel by Charlotte Burns," and again tried to settle down. It was important to concentrate, judge this as a translation from print to screen. After all, hadn't Karl Brach finally taken a small option on my own book? Which, come to think of it, had interested Herb Lobel much more than the world news or my mental state.

In fact, the adaptation was really clever, very witty and after a while engrossing. But the novel was fading further and further into the distance. Then came a scene I remembered, of Margo yielding to her lover, of her being bent back in a passionate embrace, but stopping to adjust a little bibelot on an end table before she surrendered completely. On screen there was a closeup of the lovers' faces. Then a closeup of Margo's hand reaching out. People laughed. But in the book, Margo had been straightening a crystal candy dish. Domestic comedy. Very clever. Here she was reaching for a little African figurine with a very big penis.

"Ramona called," Peter said, when I came home.

Late. I didn't say where I had been. I hardly heard him. I was wondering why Charlotte couldn't have objected to that cheap vulgarity? It couldn't have been a sell out. She didn't need the money. She could have called the whole thing off. Then I remembered that despite her professed contempt for the proceedings she had nevertheless been on the set every day.

Peter repeated that Ramona had called.

"What about?"

"I don't know, but she sounded happy," Peter said.

"Ramona's always happy," I said. "She just doesn't always know why."

It was a hurried dinner. After the chicken pot pies, though not technically Joey's turn to clean up, Peter darted off to a meeting. He seemed to be always darting off to meetings lately. Then Melissa announced that she had to go home early. Her mother needed her for something, she told me, making a face. God knew what.

"Well, when you're married and have children, too—" I began automatically.

"Oh, I'm never getting married and having children," Melissa said.

"Really? When did that come over you?"

"Lately."

The idea bothered me more than I would have expected. What did I care whether Melissa got married or not? Was I thinking about poor smitten Joey?

"But why shortchange your life?" I asked. I thought a moment. No, I could hardly tell her life was a football field. "I mean, practically speaking, all we're really sure of is that we get one crack at it. So why eliminate an entire profound area of experience?...And what about love?"

"What about it?" Melissa said.

Good question. "It taps you on the shoulder when you're not looking."

"It's not going to tap my shoulder," Melissa said shaking her great mop of hair as she headed off.

I wondered if maybe I should consult that list of shrinks, after all. Joey aside, Melissa was reminding me more and more of myself when I was young. And what could I tell her with absolute certainty, and without fear of contradiction? That the dilemmas of womanhood would be all solved by the time she grew up? This hardly seemed to me a safe prophecy anymore. But that meanwhile, until the bets were all in, not to take any crap from anybody? I wasn't exactly a role model in this area. And it was hardly something to cross stitch on her sampler. Don't Take Any Crap from Anybody. In fact, that was more Charlotte's motto than mine. But how much crap had she taken? A cheap and vulgar scene in a movie didn't necessarily mean anything.

Ramona finally caught me the next day, chirping away ecstatically. Mort Glasgow had read that piece of the third book and wanted to talk. Wasn't that fabulous? Mort Glasgow? "You sent that little piece of manuscript to him? But he was Charlotte's editor."

"Former," Ramona reminded me, "ex," clearly wondering why I too wasn't jumping for joy. I tried to stall, think it over. "What about Crutchworth? Doesn't he have an option?" I asked. "Lish, dear," Ramona said sweetly, "you're in a whole other league now."

Mort Glasgow was certainly an impressive figure, even more so at the Four Seasons, legendary home of so many publishing lunches, than he had been at the funeral. Tall and very attractive in an old-fashioned snaggle-toothed Yale way, he fit in perfectly. I had never been here before, and chances were I never would again. Crutchworth considered instant coffee in his office a remarkable feat of hospitality. Charlotte had said dismissively that the Four Seasons had become a mere cruise ship. But to me it was still a luxury ocean liner, with its hovering maitre d's, a pseudo-Roman reflecting pool in the middle of the room, an atmosphere redolent of important deals being made. Definitely Charlotte's milieu, no matter what she said. I could see why Charlotte had stayed with Mort Glasgow so long. I just couldn't see why she had left him. Especially since Arlene Mott sat at a table nearby, casting a pall over some young male author. If she saw me she gave no sign of it.

"I'm sorry. I didn't hear you," I said to Mort Glasgow, as Ramona looked on, horrified. Her expression asked, how could I not have heard him?

"I was merely wondering how the idea of coming over to Scroll House strikes you."

"Well, I haven't given it much thought. You've quite taken me by surprise, Mr. Glasgow."

"Mort. Really?"

"Oh, yes, I mean, you're a legend in your own right, of course. And when I think of all the famous authors you've edited…" Suddenly I could think of only one, but he was smiling, the point having been made anyway. "Including Charlotte Burns. I heard you at the funeral."

"Including Charlotte Burns." He nodded gravely, while Ramona now looked utterly appalled, as if our train had taken off in a completely wrong direction.

"I wonder if you know that Vanity Fare wasn't her first attempt at a novel," he asked me, making it sound more like a statement than a question. "There were two others, never finished."

"I didn't know that."

"Ah, yes. But Vanity Fare was a different matter from the start. We worked on it together. Very closely, for months. I saw immense possibilities there immediately."

Possibilities? Worked on it together for months? Was he suggesting that the book was a collaboration? Charlotte had never hinted at such a thing. On the other hand, she had been very reluctant to talk about Vanity Fare at all.

"And you see 'immense possibilities' in my manuscript too?" I said delicately.

"Lish, I wouldn't be here if I didn't. Especially since I sense in it the beginnings of a fascinating a struggle between a young writer and an established one."

"That was just a subplot beginning to creep in."

"Maybe we can get it to stand up and walk."

"Mort's an editor in the great tradition," Ramona rushed in to say. "He works hand in hand with his authors."

"Some of my authors, the ones I'm most interested in," Mort Glasgow said, raising an inquiring eyebrow at me.

"Of course, I should be talking about contracts, advances, publicity budgets and all the rest of that, and I will," Ramona burbled. "But Scroll House carries with it so much prestige in the literary world that I feel—"

It was hard to say which of us she was trying to sell, since she was looking ardently at each of us in turn.

"Naturally, I can't commit yet, not until I see much more. Let's just say that if we're both satisfied with the results Scroll House will be prepared to back you all the way," Mort Glasgow said.

Oh, yes, I was indeed in another league from Crutchworth and Sons. My complaints about Crutchworth were that they left you completely on your own to sink or swim, mostly to sink. Here, I was being approached by an editor who thought he was Maxwell Perkins and earnestly desired to take me in hand. (In more ways than one, I began to suspect. As he had with Charlotte, too?) It was all very seductive, as was Glasgow himself. That gorgeous breeding, the slender fingers breaking up his roll, the nasal voice capturing each syllable and bending it to his will. I had often dreamed of being asked to prostitute my talent, but never figured out how I would answer. Now I could see the attractions of succumbing to the whole package, this four star restaurant, the promise of fame, Mort Glasgow himself. But it was also like being in a time warp. A Star is Born. Were they still born this way? And what if the new book (as yet untitled, not to say mostly unwritten, though the subplot did have a certain new fascination for me too) failed to fulfill his expectations, what if Reunion was panned, what if Karl Brach threw in the sponge on the film/movie? After all, many were optioned, but few were chosen. I had a feeling that in any of these worst case scenarios, Mort Glasgow would beat a very hasty retreat, albeit a very polite one. I was way out of my depth. Lost. And Ramona was too hot on the trail to give me a hand. I was probably her first author to get this near to the literary big time, no matter how. If I flopped, so would she. And she had worked hard for me in her way. Where was Charlotte, when I needed her, I thought absurdly. This was Charlotte's turf. Above all, I had to know how much of Vanity Fare Mort Glasgow had actually been responsible for.

"To get back to Charlotte Burns for just a moment—" I began.

Both Ramona and Mort Glasgow cocked their heads at me. That was another time and another country, they were both telling me silently. They didn't need to add the last line, which for different reasons we were all thinking anyway.

"I missed you at the last PEN Club meeting," Sam Cuccio said, calling some days later, with his unerring instinct for knowing the exact moment in the morning when Joey and Peter left the house.

"You weren't at that meeting."

"That's how I missed you."

"Oh, Sam, for god's sakes."

The awful part was that I had started to miss him too. The last person I ought to be involved with. But even his voice reminded me touchingly of another time, when all my problems were simple, gushy, girlish. By now I didn't doubt that he and Charlotte had a history together. But what was it? Why had she warned me against him. What an irony. After all those times I had wanted desperately to talk to Charlotte about Sam, here I was desperate to talk to Sam about Charlotte.

"Look, Sam," I said, temporizing. "I'm not interested in any more tea parties."

"I had no intention of asking you to a tea party," he said in an injured voice.

"No?"

"Not all. This time I thought we might go farther up Fifth Avenue, to a museum."

"The Guggenheim?" I said warily.

"That 'awful bunker'? Of course not. Or am I not quoting you correctly?"

"You are."

"Well, then, that's why I thought of the Frick. Unless you hate the Frick too?"

"You know I don't."

Damn it, why did I keep falling for this when I knew better? But Sam had done it again, picked another place of the kind I had once only dreamed about in Forest Hills. That elegant mansion, that lovely lawn unrolling behind elaborate wrought iron gates. When Joey was very little and my mind was turning to mush, I used to come clear across the Park, Joey and stroller included, and sit on a bench opposite, just for the sheer pleasure of looking at the beautiful facade, and to remind myself that there was life above and beyond goddamned Dr Spock. I never went inside. Pushing a stroller around even if the rules had allowed it, would break the spell. Charlotte had probably never pushed a stroller.

"Thursday afternoon? Friday?" Sam said. "I won't suggest lunch because I know that interrupts your work day."

What work day? My work days were now a shambles, one false start after another. But, "Sam," I said, "I can't. I really can't." Can't what, though? Ask you if you ever had an affair with Charlotte? Have an affair with you, myself? But the guy had never laid a glove on me.

"I'll assume Thursday," Sam said, as if I hadn't spoken, and laughed. "That seems to be our lucky day."

This time I deliberately lingered on the Fifth Avenue side of the mansion. The entrance was around the corner and I was determined that he would get there first. For some moments, I again admired the gates, the carpet of lawn, wondering what it would have been like to

VANITY FARE

be a Miss Frick, myself, exit through the French doors and descend the graceful steps between two stately gray stone urns. I was designing myself an elaborate tea gown of rose chiffon—luckily it had been an era for figures like mine—when it dawned on me that with all my stalling Sam might already not only have come but gone. I hurried around to the side entrance. Inside, the interior courtyard was as lush and silent as a hothouse, and as empty of human habitation. The little pool in the center placidly reflected the surrounding pots of ferns and other foliage, but nothing else. Then I saw Sam at the far end, looking through an arched doorway into one of the galleries. His back was turned to me. He was dressed, ominously, all in black. Black turtleneck sweater, black trousers. A black jacket hanging from a thumb. Danger, danger, danger. The Mafia at the Frick. I asked myself what the hell I really thought I was doing here, and kept advancing nevertheless. Abruptly the man in black turned around, and became Sam. Smiling, beguiling, handsome Sam Cuccio.

"Alicia, how nice," he said, holding out his arms, which I entered. He gave me a kiss on the check and gently disengaged me. "Look," he said, pointing through the doorway at a statue in the next room. "Diana the huntress."

I looked at the statue, then at Sam, suspiciously. It was a naked female in bronze, holding a bow but no arrow. Was this the prelude to some macho remark? None came. Instead he beckoned me into the gallery, where we strolled around in a companionable and on my part fraught silence, gazing at various beautiful lords and ladies dressed in satin. Gainsboroughs. After a while we drifted into the next gallery. This one was long and skylit, the floors covered with Persian carpets, the walls lined with masterpiece after masterpiece, none of which I seemed to be capable of focussing on, since the same thing was happening as did whenever I was near him. Sam's sheer physical proximity had turned my mind to Jello. It was terribly wrong to feel like this. A betrayal of my deepest feminist principles. I reminded myself that I was only here to find out about Charlotte. And stopped in front of a Vermeer and forced myself to concentrate on it.

In normal life I loved Vermeer. This one was called "Mistress and Maid." The mistress was wearing a yellow velvet jacket bordered in ermine, pearls at her ears, pearls entwined in her hair. The glowing colors, the textures were tangible. She was writing a letter while the maid looked on.

"It's a love letter," Sam said, appearing at my side.

"How would you know that?"

"It says so in the catalogue."

I glanced at him quickly, then pretended to study the painting again, this time with a critical eye, though I had lost all my critical faculties long ago.

"You seem very fond of this one," Sam remarked, after a while.

"I'm fond of all the Dutch interiors."

"They're very literary."

"I'm very literary."

"I know," Sam said, with a little laugh.

We finally left the Vermeer and went through the rest of the galleries in a kind of loose lockstep, Sam stopping at paintings, such as the huge Turner landscapes—were they not literary?—which he seemed to know very well. In fact he seemed surprisingly familiar with the whole museum and occasionally told me in advance what we would see next. Had Charlotte also been taken on this survey of art history? We passed through a room in which the French windows I had admired from the street now presented a view of the garden. It was easy again to imagine myself a Miss Frick, beautifully gowned, only this time on the inside looking out. I waited for Sam to come up and ask me why these French windows interested me, but when I looked around he was gone. I found him in the Fragonard Room, surrounded by a series of canvasses painted for Madame du Barry. He was admiring a little statue of a satyr and two bacchantes. One of the bacchantes was lolling back and the laughing satyr was tweaking her tit. Sam was smiling as at an old favorite. He saw me and abruptly glanced at his watch. Oh, God. Was history repeating itself? Would I be out on the street again within a matter of minutes? But no.

"Can I possibly persuade you to change your mind about tea?" Sam asked, to my surprise.

"Oh. Well, actually I—"

"Wonderful. Would you mind if we had it in my studio? It's just down the block."

His studio. I looked at him, but he was the picture of innocence, if that could ever be said of Sam Cuccio. We left the Frick, walked the half block to Madison Avenue, which was the first time we had ever walked out on the street together—a fact I found oddly moving—then crossed over to an elegant gray townhouse. Unusual place for a studio, but what did I know about it? There was no name at all on the doorbell. Sam let himself in with a key from a large set. It suddenly dawned on me that this was his house, that the whole place belonged to him, that he lived here. But what about his wife? And his children, including the infant? Wouldn't they be home? On the other hand, why should it bother me whether they were home or not? They had nothing to do with the purpose of this meeting, which was, to repeat, to find out about Charlotte. We stepped into a small vestibule—I glanced down the hall at what seemed to be a formal diningroom, complete with floral centerpiece—and took a tiny wallpapered elevator to the top floor. The elevator opened, surprisingly, onto what looked like a separate apartment, comfortably furnished bachelor style, with a leather sofa, deep armchairs, a rug, bookcases, and a large desk laden with a big IBM Selectric typewriter and stacks of manuscript. On the opposite wall was a long kitchen counter and a complete set of unused appliances.

"You can have tea if you want," Sam said, stepping behind the counter and rummaging around, "and if I can find the damn teapot. Personally, I'm having a martini."

Which once again proved that the afternoon at the Plaza was the only time he'd had tea in his life. "I'll pass on the martinis," I said.

"They're awfully potent. I'll just have some—"

"Does potency frighten you?" Sam said, with that, yes, wicked grin.

Our eyes met. I couldn't answer. It was like a mini Cuban missile crisis. I was the one who blinked.

Sam made two martinis and put one in front of me. He came around the counter and pulled up a stool. We were sitting knee to knee. What the hell. I took a small sip, then another.

"You're so suspicious, Alicia," Sam said gently. "Hasn't it occurred to you that I'm lonely, and that this wasn't the first time I've wandered around in the Frick? That I spend much of my working day in solitary confinement, just as you do?" I looked over at his desk. The IBM typewriter and the big piles of paper had been reassuring from the beginning. Of course he didn't mention his wife and kiddies, but they wouldn't alleviate the solitude of which he spoke anymore than Peter and Joey did mine. I sighed. Yes, the silence could be deafening.

He filled my martini glass again, since I seemed to have finished the first. It wasn't really potent. There was just a slight burning down my throat and then an extraordinary soothing warmth all over my body. The sensation was familiar. I was beginning to get drunk. When had I felt this before? Suddenly I remembered and put my drink down firmly.

"I have a portable," I said, "typewriter, that is. Because I work in the dining room, and have to clear everything away afterward. When I finish."

"Ah." Sam took my hand. "Yes, tell me about your work. How's it going? I heard Karl Brach optioned the last one for a movie."

Word did get around, I thought, transfixed by his steady dark eyes. "Yes, and also I have this new one. Book. Really just started. Mort Glasgow is interested—Charlotte's editor? Former."

"I know who Glasgow is. Good for you."

"Yes, but the problem is—"

VANITY FARE

He kissed me lightly on the lips. "Oh, Sam," I murmured, trying to remember what the problem was.

"Yes, darling?" His breath was hot in my ear.

"You don't give a damn about my work."

"Don't I?"

"Do you?"

Now his hand was trying to get inside my dress.

"Do you give a damn about mine?" he whispered.

"No, I hate it," I whispered back.

So what if Charlotte had slept with him? He wasn't her personal property. And she was the one who had betrayed me, not the other way round. Anyway, this was beginning to have nothing to do with Charlotte. Nothing at all. No, this was like a Dr. Seuss book I used to read to Joey, On Beyond Zebra, about all the imaginary letters of the alphabet after Z. Beyond words. Beyond language. Beyond anything. This.

Sam had started to lead me to the leather couch. "Sam," I said falteringly, "this wasn't the purpose of my visit."

"Of course not. Are you on the pill, darling?"

"No. I mean, I used to be. But new findings show it can lead to strokes. I think it was Nancy Tarkov, who—"

"Fascinating," Sam said. "Fascinating." He lowered me gently, stroking my hair. Should I mention that I had a diaphragm, which, naturally, I had left at home? Was that relevant?

Sam sat up with an abrupt sigh. "You're tense, Alicia," he said. He was looking suddenly much older.

"I know... I'm sorry. I—"

He rose and went to open the door to what was evidently a bathroom. "Why don't you go in there, Alicia. and have a nice bubble bath?"

"A what?"

"It will relax you."

A bubble bath? He wanted me to take a bubble bath? Had he also put Charlotte in a bubble bath? I followed him stupidly into the john where he took a pink beribboned jar from a glass shelf and handed it to me. He blew me a kiss as he closed the door discreetly. I stood there staring at the jar and then at the tub. Could he possibly know what he was doing? I was tense. He was right about that. I looked at the jar again. It was all so French, so cinematic. And Sam was obviously experienced in these matters, much more, God knew, than I. Through the door, I heard him talking—but not to me. He was on the phone. How could he be talking on the phone at such a moment, and to whom? I realized from the chatty, easy tone, it was his wife. I stuck the bubble bath stuff on the shelf and marched back out. This wasn't French. It was Gold Diggers of 1933. Maybe Charlotte's era, but not mine. Sam calmly hung up the receiver, as I emerged.

"I'm leaving," I said.

"Is it terror or principle, darling?" Sam asked, handing me another martini, which I drank at once.

"Both."

"You're better than that," Sam said. He tried to take me in his arms. I struggled away.

"Alicia, why are you doing this to us?"

Us. Why are you doing this to us? Again I heard a dim echo, of something, somewhere. Was there an us? Did Sam think of us as an us? I stared at him. Suddenly the thought of us moved me profoundly. My head reeled. We were an us. Now I was back in his arms. I closed my eyes, and Sam kissed them. Then my cheeks, my throat, my lips...But I had to know.

"Sam, what broke up your affair with Charlotte?"

He kissed me again, automatically, then drew back, horrified. "You think I had an affair with that scrawny hag?"

"Scrawny hag?"

"Not you, darling. You're plump and fully packed. Delicious...Now, wouldn't you like to have my baby?"

VANITY FARE

His baby! Was he out of his mind? I opened my mouth and screamed, "No!"

Probably I was still screaming, as he gathered up my things and ushered me gently out the door, putting a finger over his lips.

I was surprisingly glad when, a few days later, Rhoda Garfunkel called, suggesting lunch. True, I had been neglecting her. In fact, I had forgotten all about her. But she had been my first fan, my only fan, a dependable boost, however misguided, for my self esteem. Maybe she would even be able to get my mind off the fiasco with Sam. Though if he really hadn't had an affair with Charlotte, why had Charlotte warned me against him? Could it have been pique rather than generosity?

"Look, I'm sorry we've been of touch," I apologized to Rhoda, "but an awful lot has been going on."

"I can imagine," Rhoda said.

No, she couldn't.

"Anyway, lunch would be great. It will be like old times. We'll go to the Columbia Faculty Club. Okay?"

"Sure, why not?" she said.

Her casual attitude was surprising. True, being spouses, we came to the Faculty Club only as second class citizens. But the Club itself had a first class aura, like a diner in a forties movies, complete with white table cloths, gleaming silverware, ancient Negro retainers balancing large trays on upended palms. Through the windows the long distance view was magnificent, never mind what was going on in the actual mean streets below. It really was great to be back here with Rhoda. I was looking forward to telling her about all the impressive professional events in my life, listening to her ooh and ah, myself being extremely modest in response. Naturally, there was much of an unprofessional nature I would leave out.

"Shall we have Manhattans?" I said, giggling. It was the drink we always used to have. Sweet as hell. With Rhoda it was so easy to step back in time, not to say actually regress.

"No. I'll just have some water."

"Water?" I looked around at the waiter, and decided to stick with water too. Considering what had happened the last time I had cocktails, or rather, what hadn't happened, it was a good idea.

"You can go ahead and enjoy yourself, though," Rhoda said, still mysteriously detached.

"That's all right."

Old times returned, however, in our food order. Chicken a la king, which came to us as a familiar glutinous white mass on brown toast, interspersed with pimentos, blobs of chicken, and very bright green peas. I couldn't help thinking it was a sight which would have sent Charlotte Burns running for cover. But I liked it. It tasted good.

"I guess you're very pleased with yourself these days," Rhoda said, mistaking my look of satisfacton.

"Not with myself. With certain professional areas, yes." I smiled.

But there was something still not right about the way Rhoda was listening, something downright cool. This was totally uncharacteristic. In the past nothing had been able to quell Rhoda's sweet empathetic fervor. Even when the riot cops were breaking up the anti-Vietnam student demonstrations on campus, she had felt sorry for the horses.

"Of course, it's been a difficult time too." I hesitated. What the hell. "A friend of mine committed suicide... Charlotte Burns?"

"That's right. You mentioned she was your friend."

"Yes, a very close friend. I even dreamed about her when she died. At the very hour she died, in fact." Feeling guilty, but on a roll—this was Rhoda, after all—I told Rhoda about the football field, the scurrying mice, the dulcet voice in the ether. "Then, when Peter woke me up and told me Charlotte was dead, I wasn't surprised at all. I just said, 'Of course.' Isn't that amazing?"

But I'd wasted my time. For once, Rhoda failed to lap it all up, be deeply impressed by the celebrity status my dead friend had conferred on me. Except for an absent smile, she had no reaction at all. I had sold out for a mess of pottage—considering the chicken a la king, almost

VANITY FARE

literally. But why had Rhoda suggested lunch in the first place? Certainly not for the usual reasons. I looked down, poked cautiously around among my chicken blobs, peas and pimentos, which were now getting more and more oleaginous. When I looked up again, Rhoda was gazing upon me as if I were some kind of artifact. It was similar to the gaze Melissa often trained on me. I kept forgetting that Melissa had emerged from Rhoda's gene pool.

"Melissa admires you a lot," Rhoda said, reading my mind.

"Oh well." I shrugged modestly and laughed. "I'm sure that will change. She's only a kid."

"You have to be very careful what you say to kids."

"What did I say?"

"Oh, you know… 'Society has rules about women that beg to be broken.' 'Say what you were put on this earth to say.' 'Don't take any crap from anybody.' 'Over and out.'"

Had I really said all that? Wasn't the crap quote from Charlotte? "Well, all of it's open to interpretation, of course. I never meant to be taken literally," I assured her.

"I should hope not."

"Now, how about some dessert?" I asked, trying to change the subject, wanting to salvage at least a little of the old relationship, in which forbidden desserts had played a great part. "I'm afraid of gaining weight, as usual, but I will if you will."

"I'll be gaining weight with or without dessert," Rhoda said.

"No, you won't. Not if you—Oh, Rhoda!"

She had just thrown me a big curve. Literally. She looked at me, wary of how I would react. "Oh, Rhoda," I repeated, taking her hand, which she grabbed back, clearly suspecting a trick. When asked, she grudgingly said she was due in November.

Then, over my objections, Rhoda paid the check, though we had always gone Dutch before. Out on the street, having permitted me a peck on the cheek, she walked away, authentically pregnant, tremendously proud of herself. What the hell was she so proud of? My god, I could have been impregnated now too, for that matter, an experience involving a celebrity that I knew enough this time not to share with her. Didn't she realize that she had actually copped out? Solved her problems by starting them all again from scratch? What would she have going for her when this one left the nest? I would have been sorry for her, if I weren't so angry. And if she hadn't been so clearly sorry for me.

I had gone through the galley proofs weeks before. Now actual copies of Reunion were stacked up on different tables around my living room. The ten free ones I had received from my publisher, the twenty-five extra I had ordered at half price and didn't know what to do with. The books should have been a miraculous sight, the fruit of intense years of labor. That was how it had been with the first one. This time, I just felt queasy. At first I put it down to the chicken a la king, but it got worse when I looked at the author's photograph on the back cover. There I was, an overstuffed mummy coming out of the black Bergdorf dress I had once insanely thought was flattering, with a surprised look on my face, as if I knew my boobs were about to fall out completely. I thanked God it was only in black and white, not full color. While I was at it, I also begged Him not to let the Times run it along with the review, if they ever did review it, but use the other picture Crutchworth's publicity department had sent them instead, of overweight, literary me in a grim, tailored suit. This assumed that I was important enough for the Times to run my picture, which was also in doubt. I seemed to be in the dark about so many things.

I went into Joey's room, relieved to find him alone. There he was, a picture of innocence, listening to cacophony through earphones, the volume so high I could hear the tinny seepage where I stood. Thank God, Melissa wasn't around, for a change. Only my sweet boy, eyes closed, nodding rhythmically, sneakered feet splayed out. I decided I ought to say something to him on the subject of Melissa while I had this chance, though I didn't know what. But, considering my conversation with Rhoda, I was beginning to feel it was my innocence that was at stake here.

Joey looked up at me inquiringly, alerted to my presence by my looming shadow. "I'd like to talk to you, Joey."

"Sure. What about?"

"Unplug yourself first." Agreeably, he removed the earphones, but I still didn't know where to start. I saw Reunion lying on the floor, half hidden under a pile of dirty clothes and an old skateboard. His personally inscribed copy. "For Joey, with all my love always. Your Ma."

"Is that where you keep it? I asked, pointing.

"Gee, it must have fallen down. I was looking for it," Joey said hastily, fishing the book out. He glanced at the back cover and blushed beet red. Then he stuck Reunion front cover up on a corner of his littered desk.

What are you blushing about?" I said.

"Blushing?"

"Just because I'm your mother doesn't mean I can't be a woman, does it?"

"No. Yes."

He was blushing harder. I had the poor kid on the ropes, and I hadn't even got to the point yet, any point.

To my horror, Melissa chose that moment to emerge from Joey's bathroom, where she seemed to have been all the time. "Hi, Lish," she said pleasantly, settling next to Joey on the studio couch and picking up my book from the edge of his desk. She turned it over and began to study the back cover. Though Joey's window was open to the breeze, I had begun to sweat.

"Boy, I really have to hand it to you," Melissa said admiringly. "You've got so much passion, Lish. And you're not afraid for people to know it. I mean look at this fearless display of your breasts, your femininity. Another woman might have—"

I closed my eyes

In her case it wasn't much of a chest. Experience wasn't going to exactly profit. Had Joey?

"Go home, Melissa," I said.

Melissa looked at me as if she hadn't heard right.

"Go home and try not to come back," I said.

"What are you talking about, Ma?" Joey cried.

"I'm talking about Melissa's mother. I'm talking about me. I'm talking about…" What the hell was I talking about?

"She looks funny," Melissa said.

I bolted down the hall to my own bathroom, slamming the door and clutching my middle. When my cramps had subsided, I looked down and saw that the water in the toilet bowl was bloody. A normal monthly event. I had my period. Rhoda was pregnant. I didn't envy her. God no. I didn't want to be pregnant. That wasn't it. But nevertheless I felt bereft as I looked down at that wasted blood, felt that wasted pain. Barren. Empty. Forlorn.

.

9

Spring was now giving way to summer, and the air was sweet. I stood in the kitchen doorway, observing my husband as he washed iceberg lettuce at the sink, his hair tipped with gold by the late sun coming in from Riverside Drive. For some mysterious reason he had gone back to making the salad, and was now shaking out the water one leaf at a time, then dropping it on an already soaked paper towel on top of other wet lettuce—thus insuring that the entire salad would be a wilted mess. That wet mess had become very dear to me. I felt I had nearly lost it. I would have gone on watching except that the elegant (and expensive)wristwatch I had recently bought him with some of Karl Brach's option money was being endangered by the splashing faucet. I took the rest of the lettuce gently from Peter's hand and laid it aside.

"I'll take care of this, darling, don't worry about it."

"Are you sure?"

"Absolutely." I wrapped my arms around him, and kissed him in a big way.

He kissed me in a small way and unwrapped my arms. "Lish?"

"Yes, darling?"

"Did you ever decide about going to a shrink?"

I stepped back. "Whatever makes you ask such a question?"

"Herb said you had a drink with him to discuss it."

So much for doctor/patient confidentiality. Except that Herb had me on a technicality—he wasn't my doctor. More to the point, so much for romantic interludes at the Stanhope. It hadn't been my imagination. Herb was just covering his butt, not uncharacteristically.

He had been doing it ever since we met, which was probably just as well.

"I decided against it," I said. "Too much money, and frankly I think they only create trouble. I mean, look at Charlotte—"

Why had I said that? It was a subject I always tried to avoid now with Peter, I held my breath, but Peter only asked, wiping his hands on a dishtowel and tossing it aside:

"Can we have dinner early? Herb and I are doing that joint seminar tonight."

"Of course." I had forgotten. I had designed an altogether different scenario for the evening since Joey was off having dinner and doing homework with a male schoolmate, Scott Zuckerman. On the slimmest of pretexts—hadn't Myra Zuckerman and I gone to Forest Hills High School together?—I had called and checked that it actually was Scott Zuckerman, hating myself every minute.

"What time's the seminar?"

"Eight. But I have to be there at seven-thirty."

"Maybe I should sit in. It sounds fascinating. We could come back and have dinner after."

"Lish," Peter said. "An extremely untalented graduate student will be delivering a very long paper on suppressed sexuality in Thomas Carlyle's Sartor Resartus."

Ah. "Still, how untalented could she be? I mean the graduate student."

"He. Very."

"It's a he—?"

"Lish," Peter said.

"Okay, okay…"

Peter left the salad in my charge and went off to his study. With Joey away, I had been planning something along the lines of a candle lit feast a deux accompanied by an excellent white wine: cold boeuf en gelee, which was still not jellied, preceded by a curried chicken broth, as yet unmade, and accompanied by asparagus vinaigrette, which was awaiting the vinaigrette. Instead of which, I dried the lettuce, pushed aside the Pouilly Fusee chilling in the fridge, took out some frozen French fries and frozen hamburger, stuck them on the counter, and poured myself a glass of leftover red plonk. Then I followed Peter into his study. Peter wouldn't mind my turning up there. At one time, early in our marriage, we had even shared a study. Very happily. Maybe we could do that again. The dining room table was losing its charms.

Peter had switched on his goose neck lamp and, still standing at his desk, began to shuffle through papers. There was a famous picture of John F. Kennedy in just such a posture. It was a real turn on. The sexy intellectual lost in thought. I started to mention the similarity then stopped because Peter was clearly preoccupied. On the other hand, he did frown at the glass of red wine I was holding, as he did these days whenever I had a drink. He never made an issue of it, though it was clear what he was thinking. How could it not be?

"Want some wine too? I'll get it for you."

"Not now," Peter said, with another glance in my direction. Oddly, I was grateful for his quiet concern, which once would have bugged me. Now it seemed admirable, evidence of a calm mind in a troubled world. I wanted to keep that calm undisturbed, to cherish it, in fact. To this end, besides trying to make interesting meals, (cookbooks to pore over were stacking up in the john), I had also resolved to be more careful about Peter's laundry, lose fewer sox, make sure his suits came back from the cleaner immaculate and properly pressed in their plastic bags. The other day at Saks, ignoring a fabulous sale on dresses, I had even gone straight up to the men's department to pick up a sweater, a silk tie, a dress shirt, a few handkerchiefs. Naturally, I picked up a few things for Joey too, he was our son and I loved him, but he would be going off to college with a sex life all his own business, and then it would be just Peter and me. Peter and me.

Peter was looking extremely golden again, bent over his desk, wrapped up in his quiet dedication to his students. The elegant wrist watch on that very strong male hand, which was resting on a pile of blue books, was another big turn on.

"You're not hungry yet, are you darling?" I murmured, nuzzling his neck.

"I beg your pardon?'

In answer, I smilingly pulled down the zipper on Peter's sweet, sweet fly, and reached inside his trousers. "Hey, wait a minute, Lish—" But I urgently pulled him over to his studio couch. "Come on, Peter, let me make love to you," I said. "What?" "Please, Peter, I want to make love to you." More curious than surprised, he lay back, and I did make love to him, slavishly, as if he were a movie star in a teenage daydream. And he let me. In the light from the desk lamp I looked down at Peter's handsome face, watched the lids close over his blue eyes, squeeze shut, open again with astonishment at my fervor. Oh, it was bliss. I kissed him all over, licked him, stuck my finger in every orifice, sucked his slender prick until it was long and hard and I could stick it up inside me. Straddling him, I moved my hips up and down, gyrating, twisting, my hair falling over his face, until he shuddered and exploded. I didn't come. That didn't matter. I was filled up, made whole. Thank you, God.

"Thank you, Peter," I said aloud.

"That's okay," Peter said, and shifted me off him.

In the morning, a normal Peter ate a breakfast of cornflakes and milk, pecked me on the cheek, and went off to school. Likewise Joey, except that he wolfed down five blueberry muffins and a quart of orange juice. He didn't mention that Melissa was much less in evidence lately. Maybe she had gotten too much for him and he was relieved. I made myself another cup of coffee and sat at the kitchen table, remembering the hungry seduction scene in the study, and wondering whether my whole sex life with Peter from now on would be based on gratitude. Wondering if it had always been.

On my third cup of coffee, I was also wondering if, my book,

VANITY FARE

Reunion would ever be reviewed in my lifetime. It was a question I had already asked myself too many times to count, and was thinking about giving up altogether when, mirabile dictu, a messenger arrived with a large manila envelope, unquestionably addressed to me. It was Tuesday, and the envelope contained an advance copy of the Sunday Times Book Review, which had been sent not by my agent Ramona, who would take a week to get around to it and talk us both blue before that, but by Mort Glasgow. A charming and seductive gesture. Clever too. I would always remember gratefully that he taken the trouble. I also understood that he would never have sent the review if it had been lousy. Nevertheless my heart began to pound unbearably as I fumbled through pages. Sex, laundry, gourmet cooking had vanished without a trace. My mind was completely one track. Ah, there it was! Right up front. A long one. In fact, there I was. They had used the book jacket photograph, after all. But the texture was so dark and grainy no one could tell where the dress ended and my boobs began, which was all to the good. The text was even more gratifying. I was intelligent and deft and witty. I was sensitive, clever, perceptive. I was a younger novelist to watch. True, I was younger, not young, and true, the plot, such as it was, was so inaccurately summarized it didn't correspond with anything I had written, and true, the names of the characters were all mixed-up. There was also some mention of my subtle handling of Jewish undercurrents. (What Jewish undercurrents?) But the review was unquestionably a rave. Crutchworth would be ecstatic, Mort Glasgow gratified, Karl Brach not regretting his option. Incredibly, the author of this rave, which would do much to advance my career, was Nancy Tarkov. The same Nancy Tarkov, who early on had given a rave review to Charlotte Burns's Vanity Fare.

Peter was very pleased when I called him at his office to tell him about it. By Sunday lots of people were calling me to offer congratulations. Including an old friend of my mother's. My mother. "Don't let this go to your head, Allie." Old classmates, including Rhoda

Garfunkel, who, though she didn't say so, had evidently decided to be in awe of me again. Including Sylvia Maxwell, who managed to make the word felicitations sound like even more of a putdown than she had on my birthday. I wondered if I should introduce her to my mother.

Including Sam Cuccio.

"You can forget about babies, Sam," I said icily.

"What are you talking about?" he amazed and insulted me by saying. Then he added, "Listen, kid, we have to get together before you get too famous."

I hung up while he was giving me directions about how to ring the bell directly connected to his studio.

Herb Lobel had decided to give a book party for me. He was sharing expenses with Crutchworth, who was too tight to do it on his own, but it was the usual tribute to delicatessen. Some things would never change. Ramona Brill was all over the place, her mouth a faucet. Mort Glasgow sent a stunning bouquet of flowers. George Crutchworth somehow thought they were for him and kept calling Glasgow a grand gentleman of publishing. It was hard to believe that once my existence had hung on Crutchworth's every word. Reading the card on the flowers, Ramona was almost too happy to live. In fact there was occasion for another celebration, Herb told me, drawing me aside.

"I'm getting married, Lish," he said, apologetically. Adding, before I could respond, "Let's keep a lid on it for now, okay?"

He was making it our secret, for no reason I could discern. "Sure, if that's what you want."

"Well, you know, I just figured it was time to batten down my hatches," Herb explained, nervously wandering into nautical language, and sounding even more apologetic. Getting equally nervous, I wondered which girlfriend was the bride to be. It wasn't the superannuated Cuban spitfire, thank God, which would have been intolerable. Nor the literary blonde/redhead with the dead mouse inside. Nor the geisha. All of whom I now realized had been banished from the party. It was the quiet potter. Though none of the guests knew it, this was probably the last we would see of this bachelor apartment. Herb and his potter were buying big on Central Park West.

"She needs space for a studio," Herb said. "You of all people would understand that."

"Yes," I said, who was still working at my dining room table.

He laughed pointlessly.

"Mazel tov," I threw in, wondering if I would ever persuade him he hadn't let me down.

Nancy Tarkov was there too, of course. More of a star than I was. Crutchworth and Glasgow were certainly more grateful to her for her review than to me for my book. The gap between her teeth looked wider than ever as everyone cozied up to her. She was smiling at me as if we had been best friends for life. None of it made any sense. It was a dream all this, a dream I had often had. But with other characters, and the dream was realer. Even Steve Aaronson showed up, but only for a minute. Gutsy guy. I remembered him at the gathering after the funeral and knew how hard this was for him.

"I'll let you escape the cold cuts now," I said, "if you promise to take me to dinner some night soon, okay?"

"Certainly, my pigeon."

"No, I mean it, Steven. I need to talk to you."

"I know."

I went back to the party, and sat down thoughtfully on the sofa, the same one where I had once met Charlotte. In a while, Herb's fiancee came and shyly sat down beside me. She didn't know my work. What name did I write under? Would she have read anything of mine?

We chose a night when Peter was off at some Society of Fellows dinner at Columbia. Steven picked me up in a shiny new dark blue Mercedes. Before, he had driven a Cadillac, a big, doctor's Cadillac, leased not purchased, for tax purposes. This car felt bought and owned. Well, Steven Aaronson was as entitled to break with the past as anyone. For my part, I decided to forget it was a German made car and enjoy the luxury. I settled back as he headed down Broadway and over to the East Side, with the air he always had, of knowing exactly where he was going. I realized that the handsome wristwatch I had bought for Peter with some of my option money was the same kind Steven was wearing, had always worn.

I was surprised by how glad I was to see him. But he made me feel intact again, the missing pieces back in place. Protected too, for some reason. I hadn't quite realized how good looking he was, how dignified. At this close distance, though, I could see signs of aging. There had always been the distinguished touch of silver at his temples. Now his hair was much grayer, with a little rubbed out bald spot behind that I had never noticed before. There was a new suggestion of wattles under his chin. He definitely had the look of a widower.

"You're looking well, my swan," he said, expertly navigating us through Central Park.

I hesitated. "So are you."

He glanced over at me and smiled.

"Peter's out at some high level academic meeting."

"I know. You told me."

"So I thought—"

"I know what you thought, Lish," Steven said. We stopped finally at an elegant and clearly expensive Italian restaurant on Madison Avenue, not far from where he lived. He used his MD plates to park illegally.

A waiter, with much bowing and scraping, showed us to what must have been the Aaronsons' usual table. Not too near the front, not too far back, a touch secluded. "For the doctor," he said, "a Stolichnaya vodka martini. And for the lady—a double scotch on the rocks?"

"A glass of white wine," I said quickly, to make clear this was a different lady. At the waiter's suggestion we ordered the specialties of the house, whose prices Steven didn't seem to notice were astronomical. I realized now that the few times we had dined together as two couples, he had deliberately chosen restaurants Peter and I could afford. Picking up the check for us all would have been inappropriate, too grandiose. He must be a very good shrink. He was really a very thoughtful man. Well, he could afford to be. Literally. Especially with the estate Charlotte had surely left him. Still, I wondered if Steven ate out all the time now, or whether he had hired a full-time housekeeper, or whether pale wan Cynthia cooked for both of them, which was the saddest thought of all. I didn't want to pursue that now, certainly not ask questions about it. The food came. Excellent, complex, with artichokes, veal, and many expensive ingredients impossible to identify, including what I thought were truffles. I could never begin to approximate such a dish, even if my new found devotion to the kitchen had endured, which it hadn't. Nevertheless, between forkfuls, I felt impelled to say:

"You have to come over to our house for dinner one night."

"I'd love to," Steven agreed politely, though it was clearly the furthest thing from his mind.

He suddenly seemed so alone. His long face and sad eyes behind those glasses looked genuinely mournful. What would he do with his life now? I wondered again if I should tell him I had heard from Charlotte and that she was happy. Would it make him feel better or would it merely derail the evening, cause him to consider me another candidate for the hatch? Still, I could hardly postpone the subject of Charlotte indefinitely.

"Look, Steven," I said. "I really did love her, you know."

"She loved you too," he said.

That simple answer wasn't what I had expected.

"Oh, why did she kill herself? She had everything!" I blurted out. "I don't understand. She had everything. Why?"

Same stupid question I had asked Herb, a question to which Steve's answer was as good as anyone's.

"Because she wanted to."

"And what Charlotte wanted, Charlotte got?" I said. "Damn the consequences? Damn everybody around her?"

"You could put it that way if you're really angry with her," Steven said, his sad smile indicating that he wasn't. "But all Charlotte really wanted was to be loved. She needed to be loved. Nothing else really mattered."

Loved by Sam Cuccio, even if Sam, as he claimed, didn't love her back? Mort Glasgow? Karl Brach? Arlene Mott? A cast of thousands? But I had wandered into an area I certainly hadn't meant to talk about with Steven.

"She was brought up that way," Steven said. "A casualty of her generation, I guess you could say…"

Maybe. I seemed to be back in the reasons for the women's movement.

"…She couldn't have cared less how brilliant she was. In fact, it embarrassed her that she graduated summa from Gorham. That was where I first met her, you know. I was a resident at Gorham State General. She would come around. She was doing a research paper on what she considered the necessary madness of artists. Madness fascinated her. And suicide."

I could see her as an undergraduate. With barrettes in her hair, a bright lipstick smile, glossy dark brown page boy. A pleated plaid skirt, a couple of books neatly tucked under her arm. And underneath, the hardness of a diamond, a fascination with self-destruction. An irresistible challenge for the young psychiatrist who had fallen in love with her.

"We married right after her graduation."

No doubt he thought he would cure her, though he didn't say so. He did say that on their honeymoon on Cape Cod, Charlotte tried to kill herself, swimming so far out into the ocean she was almost lost from view until Steven frantically swam out and saved her. Then there were more attempts at suicide after every miscarriage—she was desperate to be pregnant—until Cynthia was born.

"Cynthia…" That pale, wan creature needing to be dragged out of the kitchen, going around pointlessly watering plants.

"Charlotte always had her heart set on what she called a real daughter," Steve said, smiling again, knowing again what was on my mind. "She kept wanting Cynthia to go shopping with her, buy pretty dresses, have tea afterward, have their hair done together—all those mother and daughter things you read about in ladies magazines."

"And then she realized Cynthia—"

"Couldn't? No, Charlotte never allowed herself to realize that. I wanted to send Cynthia to a special school. But until the end Charlotte was insisting that if only Cynthia would try..." Steven broke off.

And to think there was a time when I'd thought Sam Cuccio might be the father. If so the male chromosome would have had to step completely out of the picture. No, it had never been Sam.

"Then when Vanity Fare was published," Steve continued. "Well..."

"When Vanity Fare was published?"

But I was being stupid. To Charlotte that kind of enormous success—especially if spurious—would make her life all the more unbearable. Poor Steven. I could tell that though he probably did want to talk, he was also telling me all this because he was being kind. "Last summer in the Hamptons she tried to drown herself again."

"In the pool," I said.

"Yes."

The pool that awful Steven had tried to keep them from building. "Oh, Steven, how could you endure it?"

Another stupid question. He loved her. I could see Charlotte making her familiar little moue. "Oh, for Christ's sake, sweetie, you're not buying all this crap, are you?"

He went on to finish the story. This spring, after Nancy Tarkov's scathing review, Charlotte had gulped down a whole cache of sleeping pills. She had been immediately locked up in Mount Sinai, where her stomach was pumped out. The hospital where Herb Lobel, not Steven, was affiliated. (So he was her doctor!) I tried to imagine Charlotte among the screaming loonies. A few weeks later, she was released. Then Herb's awful party, and her drunken entrance into my house. After that, the window. I shuddered.

"You were there? In the same room?"

"Yes. Unfortunately, so was Cindy. Charlotte was…screaming…"

"Oh, God, how could she do it?"

How could anyone? How desperate would you have to be? And in how much pain?

"Don't identify, Lish," Steven said, reading my face. "You're nothing like her. Believe me. You're strong as an ox."

"Well, I'm built like one," I said.

"Oh, Lish." Steven laughed, and took my hand. I admired him so much. That he could laugh at a time like this. But deep down the man was hurting. I took the hand that still rested on mine, pressed it against my cheek, then kissed the palm. The hand, though sweet, was kind of water logged, white and freckled.

"Yes. Well, nevertheless," I said, plowing ahead. "Even though she came to my house that night, I still want to explain what happened between Charlotte and me. I don't know what she told you. But what broke us up wasn't just the simple fact that she communicated secretly with Peter about her book. It was that—"

"Communicated—is that what you call it, my swan?" Steven said wryly.

I stared at him.

"Oh, Lish, I'm sorry," he said. "I thought you—"

Knew? Was there something to know? I had always been aware of Peter's weakness for older women in distress, starting with his mother. But it was impossible to imagine him actually doing something about it—with that rooster Sylvia Maxwell, for example. And as to Charlotte…

"Steven, that can't be true. Are you sure?"

Steven looked truly sorry—for me or for himself? "No, of course not. Look, probably nothing happened… No, nothing happened…

Look, Lish, I really didn't mean to—"

My god, could this be why Peter had accused me in the bar of having driven her to suicide? Why he had slammed the door, and left me to stew in my own juice? Had he been sacrificing me on the altar of his own uneasy conscience? Suggesting, in true Peter style, that if I hadn't made trouble, hadn't upset their apple cart, whatever was in it, everything would have been all right?

"Peter said that I drove her to suicide," I told Steve, "that I killed her."

"Lish, I explained. Nobody killed her. She killed herself."

Herb Lobel had implied the same thing, but not convincingly. This came from the horse's mouth.

"But you were correct about one thing, my pigeon," Steven said, as we gathered up our things to leave. "Charlotte could get what she wanted. They're giving her the Maxwell Prize."

"The Maxwell Prize? Sylvia Maxwell agreed to give Charlotte Burns the Maxwell Prize?"

"My swan," Steven said. "You look so surprised."

But why should I have been? Charlotte's last book was not only a commercial flop, she was now a dead author.

It was late when I came home. Peter had fallen asleep in bed with the lamp on, blond hair tousled over his forehead. The Complete Works of Matthew Arnold lay propped on his stomach.

So there slept my own Ashley Wilkes. Except that he was no more Ashley Wilkes than I was Melanie, not to mention Scarlett O'Hara. Actually, I had read recently that Leslie Howard, who played Ashley in the movie, was really a Jew too, Hungarian. Which didn't mean anything except that appearances could be deceiving. And that by the same token, beneath his charming insouciant air, my Peter turned out to have a very strong schmuck component. If Charlotte had had an affair with him—which she had, why kid myself?—then the joke was on her. She had relegated herself to the graduate student category—

only too available, only too willing. Peter would never take more trouble than that. How ironic, though, that with all her fabled lovers, the only sure thing in Charlotte's erotic history was my husband, mid-level academic. But good enough to secure her the damn Maxwell Prize.

Sensing my presence, or maybe my sharp intake of breath, Peter opened his eyes and glanced at me warily. He knew I had been out with Steven Aaronson because I had told Joey where I was going, and Joey had told him.

"Nice evening?"

"Yes, very."

"Look, Lish—"

"Go back to sleep, Peter," I said.

I put out the light, but not before I had seen him give me another wary look. He'd never been wary of me before. No doubt by tomorrow he would be his old, assured self again, implying as always whenever I had an interesting idea that I was a nut case. And maybe I was. I had wanted to be Charlotte Burns. But even Charlotte Burns couldn't be Charlotte Burns because there was no Charlotte Burns. I had made her up. Had Charlotte made me up? "Oh, sweetie," I could hear Charlotte say, "how could it have been otherwise? We're both novelists." Cute and typically Charlotte—would I never stop hearing her?—but it didn't really explain anything.

Sighing, I lay down beside Peter with my clothes still on, and he instinctively cradled his head against my breast. He opened his eyes, closed them again, then burrowed deeper into my too ample bosom. Like a baby. I rested my chin on the top of his soft blond hair. So I did have a baby after all. Had had one all along.

But everything else was still up for grabs. I still didn't know whether Charlotte Burns had actually written Vanity Fare. More importantly, I still didn't know what exactly had killed her in the end. Herself, out of guilt and despair? Nancy Tarkov, with a vicious review? Me by throwing her out of my house? If so, why had she come there in the first place? What had she seen in me? A younger Charlotte Burns to love and to cherish? A new generation out to supplant her? If so, she'd been certainly wrong about that. I'd already decided to tell Mort Glasgow that nothing creeping around in my book would stand up and walk unless I wanted it to. I had neither the build (already established), nor the looks, nor the inclination to be Galatea to anyone's Pygmalion. But who Lish Lasker/Alicia Morris would turn out to be was still another mystery. This was the hardest idea in the world for someone like me to be patient with, though I would have to try.

Peter's breath was coming warm and moist and regular on my skin. The hell with it. I settled in next to him for the long haul and a short sleep. At least I knew the difference between trying and dying. That must count for something.